新文京開發出版股份有限公司

NEW
WCDP

新世紀‧新視野‧新文京 — 精選教科書‧考試用書‧專業參考書

陳愛華・張景翔

編著

實用
英文

PRACTICAL
ENGLISH

序言
PREFACE

編者的話 ☆☆☆

　　當前世界，由於科技的不斷進步，使得國與國之間的距離越來越近，而且國人出國旅遊、商務、遊學也已蔚為風潮。為了能順利達成出國目的，並結交異國朋友、深入認識異國文化，以拓展個人視野，語言能力的強化有利於達成上述需求。由於經年累月徜徉於英語教、學場域中，逐漸養成隨時自學英文的習慣，其一就是看板學英文法。舉凡在國內或國外，看到有文字的招牌看板，總會不自覺的舉頭默學，當下心中感覺滿足愉悅。遇見對英文有興趣的學生要求推薦英文字彙的書籍，想要擴增英文單字量時，我總會以個人覺得有趣味的英文單字學習方式和學生分享，那就是－看板學英文的方法，看板上顯示的訊息精簡實用，較容易快速消化並接受。本書很榮幸的邀請張景翔先生一起協助本書的完成，張先生目前在英語教育機構擔任英文線上課程顧問，於英語教學實務與應用方面有多年的經驗，特別邀請他共同編纂本書，以提供讀者在英文學習實務方面的經驗與參考。

　　許多學子英語學習多年，仍侷限在課堂的學習法，大部分的學生出了教室，英文看不懂，也開不了口。曾經帶英語系的學生去美國參訪，期間，在博物館參觀時，有一名學生竟然無視於「Photography Prohibited」二字的看板，拿著她的手機拍照，當場被工作人員制止。當下該名學生很尷尬，我詢問她立牌都已說明禁止攝影，為何沒注意？沒想到她回答說不懂 Photography Prohibited 二字的中文意思！也曾有一位同事出國回來買了保養品，原以為是護手霜，但是卻是護髮霜，類似誤解的情形不勝枚舉。讓筆者發想將國內、外蒐集的英文路標看板，集結成冊，讓讀者能以輕鬆愉快的方式學習英文。

本書特色 ☆☆☆

　　本書共分為五個部分：高鐵站、機場、訂房及餐飲、路標及校園生活等告示牌或傳單，並搭配相關的情境式對話。並在"Practice"單元每頁一張圖片，處下附上相關單字及問題，供讀者能輕鬆的學會看懂相關的英文。舉凡在學學生、出國商旅、探親、遊／留學，以及觀光旅遊或餐飲業者皆可以參閱本書。

如何使用本書 ☆☆☆

對話部分

- 讀者可以和同伴一起練習英文對話，並學習實用之單字及片語。

圖片部分

- 讀者先詳閱圖片及上面出現的文字（請先不要看中文解釋）。

- 將陌生的單字標示出來，試著自己唸出該單字或片語。

- 順著圖片往下，看相關的單字或片語的中文解釋。

- 熟悉單字或片語後，再往回看圖片，試著將圖片上的文字化為己有。

- 進階讀者：可以試著就圖片及文字和同伴編寫一小段對話，再一起做對話練習。

A: What are you going to do with this empty bottle?

B: I'll dump it. Where's the trash can?

A: Why don't you recycle it?

B: OK. I'll do it later. By the way, we are not allowed to take this road.

A: Why?

B: Don't you see the sign. It says, No Motor Vehicles Allowed. We'd better go straight until the next turn.

結語 ☆☆☆

　　各位敬愛的讀者，希望在閱讀完本書後，您的英文功力更上層樓。當您出國時，能輕鬆的看懂路邊的英文招牌、傳單或餐廳的菜單。此外，有任何寶貴意見也懇請賜教：陳愛華　ah121301@yahoo.com.tw。

目 錄
CONTENTS

I High-Speed Rail Station　高鐵站

II Airport　機場 ✈

III Accommodation & Meals　訂房及餐飲 🍽

目 錄

IV Road Signs 路標 ➡

V Campus Life 校園生活 ✏

High-Speed Rail Station

高鐵站

Lesson 1

Which car are we in?

Ding-Ding and Ping-Ping are good friends. They have known each other since they were in elementary school. They plan to go to visit their mutual friend, Manman, who is currently on an internship in the U.S. Now they are taking a taxi to the high-speed railway station.

D: After working so hard for months, it's nice that we can take our trip at last.

P: Yes, it's fun to go travelling together.

In the station hall

D: Where can we buy tickets?

P: We can buy them from the self-service ticket machine. Let's get our tickets.

D: What tickets are you getting, reservation or non-reservation?

P: I think we can get non-reservation tickets to save a few pennies.

D: OK. Now, where do we get the train from?

P: From the northbound platform. Let's go there.

Ding-Ding is walking to the escalator

P: Hey, we'd better take the elevator with our luggage instead of the escalator.

D: Oh, you're right.

P: Here we are. Which car are we going to be in?

D: The non-reserved cars are 10 through 12. How about car 12? There's nobody in there.

P: Good idea. We have to stand in line behind the yellow line.

D: How long is it until the train comes?

P: The monitor shows that the train will be approaching the platform in two minutes.

D: How long will it take to get to Taoyuan Station?

P: About 40 minutes.

D: What are we going to do after we get to the station? Do we need to take a taxi?

P: Not necessarily. It's very convenient now. We just take the MRT line to the airport.

D: That's really efficient for saving time travelling.

P: Yes, it really is. The train is stopped now. Let's get on. Watch your step!

I. **Vocabulary words and phrases**

1.	mutual	[`mjutʃʊəl]	共有的
2.	northbound	[`nɔrθbaʊnd]	北行的
3.	escalator	[`ɛskəˌletə]	電扶梯
4.	efficient	[ɪ`fɪʃənt]	效率高的

5.	high-speed railway	高速鐵路
6.	non-reservation	非保留
7.	instead of	而不是…
8.	non-reserved car	自由座車廂
9.	stand in line	排隊

II. Answering the following questions

1. How do Ding-Ding and Ping-Ping get to Taoyuan Station?

2. What type of tickets do they book?

3. How do they get to the airport from Taoyuan Station?

In Case of Emergency

Many signs are posted in places to remind passengers to be cautious. After booking the tickets and en route to the platform, Ding-Ding looks around and sees many signs. He is interested in those signs and would like to talk about them with Ping-Ping.

D: Ping-Ping, did you notice that there are many signs around?

P: Yes, I did. We still have some time. So, if you like, we can take a look at them.

D: What is the purpose of posting the signs?

P: They tell people what they can do in case of emergency.

D: Can you give an example?

P: OK. Do you see that phone on the wall? What is it for?

D: Is it a payphone?

P: No. You cannot make a personal call with it.

D: No? Then, who can use it and when?

P: Actually, it's an intercom, not a phone. In case of emergency, people open the little door and use the intercom to contact attendants.

D: Got it. I'm glad I won't embarrass myself by misusing it.

P: By the way, do you notice that most warning signs are red with white writing? I guess they attract attention better.

D: Yeah, you're right. Wherever we are and whatever we're doing, being cautious is the best policy.

P: That's right. And, if a serious accident happens, we shouldn't hesitate getting help or pressing the alarm.

D: I hope it never happens.

P: The train is coming. You are too close to the track. We'd better stand behind the line for the sake of safety.

D: Thank you for reminding me.

P: I hope we have a pleasant and safe trip.

D: We will for sure.

I. Vocabulary words and phrases

1.	post	[post]	貼出
2.	purpose	[`pɝpəs]	目的
3.	payphone	[`pefon]	（公用）投幣電話
4.	intercom	[`ɪntɚ͵kɑm]	對講機
5.	attendant	[ə`tɛndənt]	服務員
6.	embarrass	[ɪm`bærəs]	使尷尬
7.	policy	[`pɑləsɪ]	政策
8.	hesitate	[`hɛzə͵tet]	猶豫
9.	alarm	[ə`lɑrm]	警報器
10.	en route to		前往
11.	take a look at		看一看
12.	in case of		假如碰上
13.	for sure		肯定

II. Answering the following questions

1. When can people use the phone on the wall?

2. Why are most warning signs red?

3. What should people do in case of an accident?

Taking the High-Speed Rail

Ding-Ding and Ping-Ping are taking the high-speed rail to the Taoyuan Airport. They've got on the train with their luggage and are looking for their seats.

D: Finally, we're aboard. Where are our seats?

P: Well, our luggage is very big. First I think we'd better put it in the designated area and buckle it up.

D: Got it. And here are our seats. Which do you prefer, aisle or window seat?

P: May I take the window seat? I can enjoy the beautiful view.

D: Sure. Let me put our laptop on the overhead luggage rack first.

P: Everything's set. I need to go to the lavatory.

D: Don't forget to lock the door!

P: You must be kidding. Could you please watch my bag?

D: No problem.

A few minutes later, Ping-Ping returns to her seat.

P: I saw one guy who was talking on his phone very loudly. I feel embarrassed for him.

D: Indeed. There's a sign saying we should speak in low voices on phone calls. As such, we won't disturb other passengers.

P: Maybe he can't read. By the way, I found that the lavatory is quite small, but it is very clean.

D: Of course. Compared to other trains, high-speed rail charges people more so the passengers should get better service.

P: And the seating is more spacious so we can stretch our legs out.

D: Yes. Are you hungry? Would you like some snacks? There's a lady pushing a food cart and selling lunch boxes and drinks.

P: I'm fine. We can have our lunch at the airport after checking our luggage in. If you are hungry, you can get something to eat now.

D: No, I can wait. I enjoy having lunch with you.

P: The train is very fast. It should arrive at the station in ten minutes.

D: I'll take our laptop off the rack.

P: Some passengers are moving to the door. I'll follow them and get the luggage.

After getting off the train, they connect to the MRT line to the airport.

Ⅰ. Vocabulary words and phrases

1.	aisle	[aɪl]	走道
2.	laptop	[`læptɑp]	筆記型電腦
3.	overhead	[`ovɚˋhɛd]	在頭頂上的
4.	rack	[ræk]	架子
5.	lavatory	[`lævəˌtorɪ]	盥洗室
6.	indeed	[ɪnˋdid]	確實
7.	disturb	[dɪsˋtɝb]	打擾
8.	charge	[tʃɑrdʒ]	收費

9.	spacious	[`speʃəs]	寬敞的
10.	connect	[kə`nɛkt]	連接
11.	buckle up		繫好安全帶
12.	as such		因此
13.	stretch out		伸出
14.	food cart		食物推車

II. Answering the following questions

1. When people are taking the high-speed rail, where do they put their luggage?

2. Where do they put their laptop?

3. When people need to talk on their phone, what do they need to do?

Practice

I-1

1.	escalator	[ˋɛskəˌletɚ]	自動樓梯，電扶梯
2.	up-running	往上運行	

📌 Where are people going to when they are taking the up-running escalator?

I-2

請搭乘月台電梯
Please use platform elevator

 行動不便
Disabled

 年長
Elderly

 推嬰兒車
Baby stroller

 孕婦
Pregnant

 攜帶大型行李
Large luggage

1.	platform	[`plæt͵fɔrm]	（鐵路等的）月臺；平臺；講臺；戲臺
2.	disabled	[dɪs`eb!d]	殘廢的；有缺陷的
3.	stroller	[`strolɚ]	摺疊式嬰兒車；閒逛的人；巡迴演出的演員；遊蕩者
4.	elderly	[`ɛldɚlɪ]	年長的；上了年紀的
5.	pregnant	[`prɛgnənt]	懷孕的，懷胎的；意味深長的，含蓄的

Who had better use the platform elevator?

I-3

1.	arrival	[əˋraɪvḷ]	到達；到來；達到
2.	destination	[ˏdɛstəˋneʃən]	目的地，終點；目標，目的
3.	delay	[dɪˋle]	延遲；耽擱
4.	southbound	[ˋsaʊθˏbaʊnd]	往南的；南行的

📌 When is the departure time bound to 左營？

📌 What platform is it?

I-4

自由座車廂
Non-reserved car
10-11-12

1.	car	[kɑr]	火車車廂；汽車；有軌電車；（氣球，飛船，纜車）吊艙；（電梯）升降廂

2. non-reserved 非預留的；非保留的

 How many cars are non-reserved?

I-5

The floor could be wet and slippery due to the rain. Please watch your step!

1.	floor	[flor]	地板，地面；（樓房的）層
2.	slippery	[ˋslɪpərɪ]	滑的；容易滑的；（問題等）須小心對待的
3.	due to		因為；由於
4.	watch your step		留心您的腳步

📌 Why could the floor be wet and slippery?

📌 What do people need to do when walking on the wet and slippery floor?

I-6

緊急停機鈕
Emergency Stop Button

1.	emergency	[ɪ`mɝdʒənsɪ]	緊急情況；突然事件；非常時刻
2.	button	[`bʌtn]	按鈕；鈕扣，釦子

What does the sign mean?

I-7

If your ticket or any other items were to accidentally fall onto the HSR track area, please contact our station staff for assistance to retrieve the object. Under no circumstances should one enter the HSR track area. Any violation could result in a fine and/or criminal liability.

1.	item	[ˋaɪtəm]	一件物品；項目；品目；條款；細目；（新聞等的）一則，一條，一項
2.	accidentally	[͵æksəˋdɛnt!ɪ]	偶然地；意外地；附帶地
3.	track	[træk]	鐵軌，軌道；行蹤；足跡；小徑、小道
4.	contact	[kənˋtækt]	與…接觸；與…聯繫
5.	retrieve	[rɪˋtriv]	重新得到，收回；（獵犬）銜回（被擊中的獵物）
6.	circumstance	[ˋsɝkəm͵stæns]	情況，環境；情勢
7.	violation	[͵vaɪəˋleʃən]	違反；違背；違犯；違反行為
8.	fine	[faɪn]	罰金，罰款

9.	criminal	[ˋkrɪmən!]	犯罪的，犯法的；刑事上的；罪犯
10.	liability	[ˏlaɪəˋbɪlətɪ]	傾向；責任，義務
11.	fall onto		落
12.	HSR= High Speed Rail		高速鐵路
13.	under no circumstances		在任何情形下決不；無論如何不
14.	result in		導致；結果是

What do people need to do if their ticket or any other items were fallen onto the HSR track area?

In what situation can people enter the HSR track area?

What will happen to people who enter the HSR track area?

I-8

Take refuge in the recess area and shout for help if you fall onto the track.

1.	refuge	[`rɛfjudʒ]	躲避；避難；庇護
2.	recess	[rɪ`sɛs]	（山脈，牆壁等的）凹處；壁龕；休息；休會；休庭
3.	shout	[ʃaʊt]	呼喊，喊叫；叫嚷；大聲說；大聲叫

What do people need to do if they fall onto the track?

I-9

Ensure OCS(Overhead Catenary System) is powered off before using fire hydrant

1.	ensure	[ɪnˋʃʊr]	保證；擔保；使安全，保護
2.	overhead	[ˋovɚˋhɛd]	在頭頂上的；在上頭的；高架的
3.	catenary	[kəˋtinərɪ]	電氣化鐵路之架線系統；鏈狀物
4.	hydrant	[ˋhaɪdrənt]	消防栓；給水栓；水龍頭
5.	overhead catenary system		架空線系統；架空電車線系統
6.	power off		電源關著
7.	fire hydrant		消防栓，消防龍頭

🔖 What is OCS?

🔖 What do people need to ensure before using fire hydrant?

I-10

非緊急狀況請勿使用
For emergency use only

📌 What does the sign mean?

I-11

> **In case of Emergency,**
> **open the Housing Door**
> **and use the intercom to**
> **contact attendants:**
> **1. Pick up the Handset**
> **and wait for answer.**
> **2. Replace the Handset**
> **after talking.**
> **3. Close the Housing Door.**

1.	intercom	[ˋɪntɚ͵kɑm]	對講電話裝置，對講機，內部通話裝置
2.	attendant	[əˋtɛndənt]	陪從，隨員；服務員；侍者
3.	handset	[ˋhænd͵sɛt]	電話聽筒
4.	replace	[rɪˋples]	把…放回（原處）；取代；以…代替

Where is the intercom?

When do people use the intercom?

After using the intercom, what do people need to do?

I-12

如需協助，請提起聽筒與站務人員聯絡
For assistance, lift hand-set

1.	assistance	[əˋsɪstəns]	援助，幫助
2.	lift	[lɪft]	舉起；抬起；振作（精神）；提高（聲音等）

📌 When people need assistance, what can they do?

I-13

消 防 栓
HYDRANT

| 1. | hydrant | [ˋhaɪdrənt] | 消防栓；給水栓；水龍頭 |

 What does the sign mean?

I-14

Fire
Extinguisher

1.	extinguisher	[ɪkˋstɪŋgwɪʃɚ]	熄滅者；消滅者；滅火器；熄燭器
2.	fire extinguisher	滅火器；熄燈器	

What is the fire extinguisher for?

I-15

Smoking is prohibited.

| 1. | prohibit | [prə`hɪbɪt] | （以法令，規定等）禁止 |

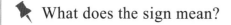 What does the sign mean?

I-16

Smoking is not permitted in this premises. Please abide by the smoke-free law.

1.	permit	[pəˋmɪt]	允許、容許
2.	premises	[ˋprɛmɪsɪz]	房宅（或辦公室）連全部建築及地基；生產場所、經營場址
3.	smoke-free	[͵smokˋfri]	禁止吸菸的
4.	abide by		遵從；遵守；承擔…的後果；承受

What is not allowed in the premises?

What is the sign for?

I-17

Escape through Windows

1. When train is stopped in case of an emergency, break the window with hammer for evacuation.
2. Vandalism will be prosecuted by law.

1.	escape	[əˋskep]	逃跑；逃脫
2.	hammer	[ˋhæmɚ]	鐵鎚，鎯頭；鎚狀物
3.	evacuation	[ɪˏvækjʊˋeʃən]	撤空；撤離；撤退；疏散
4.	vandalism	[ˋvændlɪzəm]	故意破壞公物的行為
5.	prosecute	[ˋprɑsɪˏkjut]	對…起訴；告發；依法進行

Where do people escape from in case of an emergency?

How do people escape from the window?

Why do people escape from the window?

What does vandalism mean?

I-18

● 餐桌限重10公斤。
Table Maximum Load:10Kgs.

1.	maximum	[`mæksəməm]	最大量，最大數，最大限度
2.	load	[lod]	裝載；擔子；（精神方面的）負擔

What is the maximum load for the table?

I-19

● 敬請將手機鈴聲轉成震動模式，使用手機時請輕聲通話。
Please switch your mobile phone to vibration mode and talk in a low Voice during telephone calls.

1.	switch	[swɪtʃ]	打開（或關掉）…的開關；使轉換；為…轉接（電話）
2.	vibration	[vaɪ`breʃən]	顫動；振動；震動
3.	mode	[mod]	形式，型；種類；方法，做法，方式
4.	mobile phone	行動電話	
5.	low voice	低聲	

Why do people switch their mobile phone to vibration mode?

What do people do when talking on the telephone?

I-20

This is a No Smoking Train. Smoking in any part of the train is prohibited and liable to a maximum fine of NT$ 10,000.

1. liable [`laɪəb!] 應受罰的；應服從的；應付稅的；負有法律責任的，有義務的

📌 What is not allowed in the train?

📌 What will happen if people smoke in the train?

I-21

Keep away from the Vestibule door during operation

1.	vestibule	[`vɛstəˌbjul]	火車車廂末端的連廊，通廊
2.	operation	[ˌɑpəˈreʃən]	操作；運轉；經營；營運
3.	keep away from	不靠近某人或某事物	

Why do people need to keep away from the vestibule door during operation?

I-22

Please hold the handgrip firmly if you are standing

| 1. | handgrip | [`hænd͵grɪp] | 手把；柄；有力的握手 |
| 2. | firmly | [`fɝmlɪ] | 堅固地；穩固地；堅定地；堅決地 |

While standing, what do people need to do?

I-23

> ## Use of this alarm except in the case of a safety related emergency is prohibited and can result in a fine of up to 6000NT$

1.	except	[ɪk`sɛpt]	除…之外
2.	related	[rɪ`letɪd]	有關的，相關的；有親戚（或親緣）關係的

When can people use the alarm?

What will happen if the alarm is set for fun?

I-24

You are in Car No. 11.

📌 Where are you now?

I-25

In emergency, press the red button to communicate with the train crew.

1.	communicate	[kə`mjunəˌket]	通訊,通話
2.	crew	[kru]	一組(或一隊等)工作人員;全體船員;(飛機或太空船的)全體機員,空勤人員
3.	train crew		列車車務人員

When do people press the red button?

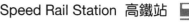

I-26

Please buckle the belt after usage.

| 1. | buckle | [`bʌk!] | 扣住，扣緊；連接；彎曲，變形；起皺 |
| 2. | usage | [`jusɪdʒ] | 使用，用法；處理，對待 |

What does the sign tell people to do?

I-27

手提行李請多利用座椅
上方行李架放置

**Please use the baggage rack for
carry-on baggage**

貴重物品請隨身保管

Please Keep your valuables with you.

1.	rack	[ræk]	架子；掛物架；（行李）網架
2.	valuable	[`væljʊəb!]	貴重物品，財產；值錢的，貴重的
3.	carry-on baggage	隨身攜帶行李	

Where do people put their carry-on baggage?

Where do people keep their valuables?

I-28

Please yield Priority Seat to pregnant women, elderly, disabled, and passengers with infant children.

1.	yield	[jild]	禮讓;讓於,結於;同意
2.	infant	[ˋɪnfənt]	嬰兒;幼兒
3.	priority seat		博愛座;敬老席

 Who can take the priority seat?

I-29

走道
Aisle

1.	aisle	[aɪl]	通道，走道

📌 What does it mean?

I-30

Maximum Load:15kgs.
Secure your baby with safety belt first.

| 1. | secure | [sɪˋkjʊr] | 把…弄牢；關緊；使安全；掩護；保衛 |

2. safety belt 安全帶

📌 What is the maximum load?

📌 How does a mother secure her baby?

I-31

嬰兒換尿布台
Baby Changing

✏ What does the sign mean?

I-32

Only dispose of toilet paper and seat-cover paper in toilet.

| 1. | dispose | [dɪ`spoz] | 處置，處理；整理 |
| 2. | seat-cover | 座椅套子 | |

What things can be disposed in the toilet?

I-33

Place your hand over the sensor to flush the toilet

1.	place	[ples]	放置，安置；投（資）；存（款）；開出（訂單）
2.	sensor	[`sɛnsɚ]	感應器
3.	flush	[flʌʃ]	用水沖洗；使（臉等）漲紅；使發紅，使發亮

Why do people need to place their hand over the sensor?

How to flush the toilet?

I-34

自動沖水器
Auto Flush Sensor

📌 What does the sign mean?

I-35

手烘乾機
Hand Dryer

What is the hand dryer for?

I-36

Please be sure to lock the door.

📌 What does the sign mean?

I-37

Spare toilet paper roll inside. When this roll is finished, pull lever to replace with a new roll. Deposit the empty roll in the trash bin, please.

1.	spare	[spɛr]	備用的;多餘的,剩下的;空閒的
2.	roll	[rol]	捲;捲狀物
3.	lever	[`lɛvɚ]	槓桿;控制桿
4.	replace	[rɪ`ples]	取代;以…代替
5.	deposit	[dɪ`pɑzɪt]	放下,放置;寄存
6.	empty	[`ɛmptɪ]	空的;未占用的;無人居住的;沒有,缺少
7.	toilet paper roll		捲筒衛生紙
8.	trash bin		垃圾桶

📌 Where is the spare toilet paper roll?

📌 How to replace with a new toilet paper roll?

📌 How to take care of the empty roll?

Airport

機場

Lesson 4

At the Airport

When Ding-Ding and Ping-Ping arrive at Taoyuan Airport, they put their luggage on a trolley and go to the departure hall.

P: Do you know where we check in?

D: Let me see. We are going to terminal two and our check-in counter is number 10.

P: There's a long line there. I'm glad we've arrived at the airport three hours before the departure.

D: It's our turn to check in.

Ground staff: May I have your passport and ticket?

D: Here they are.

G: How many pieces of check-in luggage do you have?

D: One piece.

G: Can you put it on the scale?

D: OK. Excuse me. May I have an aisle seat, please?

G: Let me see···Yes, you can. I've reserved an aisle seat for you. Here are your boarding passes. The baggage claim ticket is attached. Boarding is at gate D10. Boarding time is thirty minutes before departure.

D: Will the luggage go to the final destination? I have a connecting flight in the U.S.

G: Well, when you arrive at U.S. Customs, you have to go through an immigration checkpoint first. After that, find your luggage and put it back to the domestic baggage carousel.

D: Thank you very much.

G: Have a good trip. Your luggage will go through X-ray scanning there. You can go to check it.

After seeing the luggage successfully going through the X-ray scanning, Ding-Ding and Ping-Ping go to find something to eat.

D: Well, are you ready to go to the gate?

P: Yes. Don't forget your carry-on luggage.

D: I won't. We need to leave the luggage trolley here.

P: There are some trolleys there. Just put it with them.

D: All right. Keep your passport and boarding pass with you. Let's go now.

I. Vocabulary words and phrases

1.	trolley	[`tralɪ]	手推車
2.	terminal	[`tɝmən!]	航廈
3.	scale	[skel]	秤
4.	attach	[ə`tætʃ]	附上
5.	destination	[ˌdɛstə`neʃən]	終點
6.	Customs	[`kʌstəmz]	海關

7.	immigration	[ˌɪməˈɡreʃən]	移民
8.	checkpoint	[ˈtʃɛkˌpɔɪnt]	檢查站
9.	domestic	[dəˈmɛstɪk]	國內的
10.	carousel	[ˌkærʊˈzɛl]	旋轉木馬
11.	departure hall		出境大廳
12.	ground staff		地勤人員
13.	check-in luggage		託運行李
14.	boarding pass		登機證
15.	baggage claim		行李提領
16.	baggage carousel		行李傳送帶
17.	carry-on luggage		登機行李

II. Answering the following questions

1. Where do they check in?

2. What items do passengers provide to the ground staff at the check-in counter?

3. What do they need to do with their check-in luggage once they arrive in the U.S.?

Lesson 5

At the Security Checkpoint

Ding-Ding and Ping-Ping are standing in line waiting for the security check. They take empty X-ray baskets.

D: We're going to do the security check. I'll drink up the water to empty the bottle.

P: Ding-Ding, before going through the full-body scan, we need to take our laptop out of the backpack and put it in the basket. Also, watches, keys, batteries, and smartphones have to go in. Don't forget to take off your belt and shoes. We need three baskets to carry them.

D: OK. The backpack and carry-on luggage are ready for screening too.

They put personal belongings in the baskets and go through the body scan. Then, they take their personal items back.

D: There are so many people standing in line waiting for passport control. I'm glad we applied for the e-gate.

P: Yes. Using automated passport control kiosks saves a lot of time. Let's go and I'll see you on the other side.

D: Where are your passport and boarding pass?

P: I put them in my backpack. We'll need them later on.

They are at the departure lounge now.

D: Well, our gate is in that direction. Do you want to go there now or just look around? We still have time to shop at duty-free.

P: I'd like to buy some skin products. They are cheaper than the ones in ordinary shops.

D: OK. But don't take too much time.

P: I've got what I want. Let's go to the gate.

D: OK. Let's take a seat.

P: We're boarding in ten minutes. I'll go to the restroom first.

D: All right. I'll keep an eye on our stuff.

P: Do you want me to get some warm water for you?

D: Yes. Here's the bottle.

P: It'll be dry on the airplane. I think we need to drink more water.

D: Yes.

P: Well, it's time to board. Let's get in line.

I. Vocabulary words and phrases

1.	empty	[`ɛmptɪ]	空的
2.	backpack	[`bæk͵pæk]	背包
3.	kiosk	[kɪ`ɑsk]	捷運入口
4.	duty-free	[`djutɪ`fri]	免稅的
5.	drink up		喝完
6.	personal belongings		個人的所有物

| 7. | passport control | （出入境）護照檢查處 |
| 8. | keep an eye on | 仔細看守好 |

II. Answering the following questions

1. Why does Ding-Ding drink up the water to empty his bottle?

2. What are automated passport control kiosks for?

3. Where does Ping-Ping buy her skin products?

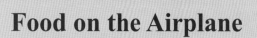

Lesson 6

Food on the Airplane

After flying for a while, the flight attendants push the trolley cart to bring drinks to the passengers.

Flight attendant: What would you like to drink, ma'am?

P: May I have tomato juice, please?

F: OK, here you are.

P: Thanks.

F: And you, sir?

D: I'd like Sprite without ice.

After serving Ding-Ding, the flight attendant continues to serve other passengers.

P: The small snack pack is very cute, and the peanuts don't taste bad!

D: If you like, you can ask for one more.

P: This is enough and we're going to have a meal soon, aren't we?

D: Yes, you can find the menu in the seat pocket in front of you.

P: That's convenient. Let me see.

It's mealtime. The flight attendants push their trolley carts to serve passengers again.

F: What would you like, chicken or beef, ma'am?

P: May I have chicken, please?

F: What beverages would you like?

P: Apple juice please.

F: How about you, sir?

D: May I have beef and wine, please?

F: Here you go.

D: Thank you.

P: Well, I'll have the bread roll with butter first.

D: The beef goes great with wine. It's delicious.

P: Don't drink too much.

D: I know. I'll have a good sleep later on.

P: This is a lot of food. I can't finish all of it. I'll save the cookies.

D: As you like. I'm full.

P: Me too. Now, we can take a good rest.

Ⅰ. Vocabulary words and phrases

1.	snack	[snæk]	零食
2.	pack	[pæk]	包
3.	beverage	[ˋbɛvərɪdʒ]	飲料
4.	trolley cart	手推車	

5.	tomato juice	番茄汁
6.	seat pocket	椅背置物袋
7.	Here you go.	這是你要的

II. Answering the following questions

1. What does Ping-Ping have to drink?

2. Where can they find the menu?

3. Why can't Ping-Ping finish her food?

Practice

II-1

Please be patient and stay in the line. Queue starts here.

1.	patient	[`peʃənt]	有耐心的，能忍受的，能容忍的
2.	line	[laɪn]	列，排；（等待順序的）行列
3.	queue	[kju]	排隊；排隊等候

📌 While people are standing in line, what do they need to be?

II-2

PLEASE PROCEED TO COUNTER WHEN GREEN LIGHT IS FLASHING

1.	proceed	[prə`sid]	繼續進行；繼續做（或講）下去；開始，著手，出發
2.	counter	[`kaʊntə]	櫃臺；櫃臺式長桌
3.	flash	[flæʃ]	使閃光；使閃爍

When the green light is flashing, what do people need to do?

II-3

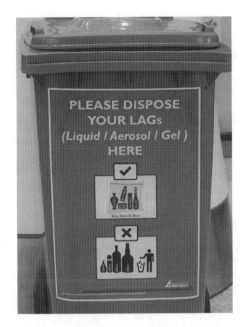

1.	dispose	[dɪ`spoz]	處置，處理；整理
2.	liquid	[`lɪkwɪd]	液體
3.	aerosol	[`ɛrəˌsɑl]	煙霧劑，氣霧劑；氣溶膠
4.	gel	[dʒɛl]	膠體；凝膠

📌 What are LAGs?

📌 What is the bin for?

II-4

SECURITY REGULATION ON
HAND LUGGAGE
FOR INTERNATIONAL BOUND PASSENGERS

You may carry Liquids, Aerosols and Gels (LAGs),
by following these simple steps:

STEP 1 Place all liquid containers in clear plastic bag-(Each liquid container should not exceed 100ml / 100gm / 3.4oz. and maximum capacity in bag is 1 litre).

STEP 2 Present all liquids in the clear plastic bag to security screening check points.

Size: 22 cm x 18 cm

Liquid items include:
- Hair gel, shoe gel, lotion, oil •Liquid-solid mixture such as pudding
- Pressurised containers such as shaving foam & deodorant •Spray •Perfume
- Water / drink, soup •Liquid consmetic •Toothpaste •Other items with similar consistency

MALAYSIA AIRPORTS DOES NOT PROVIDE THE CLEAR PLASTIC BAG.
YOU CAN STILL:
1. Pack liquids in your check-in luggage.
2. Carry baby milk, boby food, prescribed medicines with a name that matches the passenger's boarding pass, as well as insulin and other essential non-prescribed medicines.
3. Buy any liquids beyond the security check point including duty free items at shops or in-flight. items purchased must be packed in sealed / stapled plastic bag and accompanied by proof of purchase upon presenting them at the security check points.

1.	regulation	[ˌrɛgjəˋleʃən]	規章；規定；條例；管理；調整
2.	luggage	[ˋlʌgɪdʒ]	行李
3.	bound	[baʊnd]	正在前往的，打算前去的
4.	passenger	[ˋpæsndʒɚ]	乘客，旅客
5.	container	[kənˋtenɚ]	貨櫃；容器（如箱、盒、罐等）
6.	clear	[klɪr]	清澈的；（皮膚）潔淨的；晴朗的
7.	exceed	[ɪkˋsid]	超過；勝過；超出
8.	capacity	[kəˋpæsətɪ]	容量；能力，才能；資格；容量
9.	liter	[ˋlitɚ]	公升
10.	present	[prɪˋzɛnt]	展現；出現；贈送，呈獻
11.	screening	[ˋskrinɪŋz]	篩選
12.	security check point	安全檢查站	

What is the security regulation on?

Who needs to follow the regulation?

Where are the liquid containers placed?

How much can each liquid container hold?

What is the maximum capacity in one bag?

II-5

PLEASE TAKE OFF YOUR BELT OR OTHER METAL OBJECTS SUCH AS KEYS, COINS, WRIST WATCH, ETC THAT MAY CAUSE THE ALARM TO SOUND

1.	metal	[ˋmɛt!]	金屬；合金；金屬製品
2.	object	[ˋɑbdʒɪkt]	物體；對象；目標
3.	coin	[kɔɪn]	硬幣，錢幣
4.	wrist	[rɪst]	腕；腕關節
5.	alarm	[əˋlɑrm]	警報；警報器
6.	sound	[saʊnd]	發聲，響起；發音；聽起來，聽上去
7.	take off		脫去（衣物）；（飛機）起飛

Why do people need to take off their belt or metal objects?

What metal objects are mentioned?

II-6

NOTICE TO PASSENGERS

ELECTRIC OR ELECTRONIC DEVICES HAVE THE POTENTIAL OF BEING USE TO CONCEAL EXPLOSIVES DEVICES.

IF YOUR HAND LUGGAGE CONTAINS ELECTRIC OR ELECTRONIC DEVIES, DECLARE AND SEPARATE THEM AT SECURITY CHECK POINT.

1.	electric	[ɪˋlɛktrɪk]	電的；導電的；發電的；電動的
2.	electronic	[ɪlɛkˋtranɪk]	電子的；電子操縱的
3.	device	[dɪˋvaɪs]	設備，儀器，裝置；手段；謀略
4.	potential	[pəˋtɛnʃəl]	可能性；潛力，潛能
5.	conceal	[kənˋsil]	隱蔽，隱藏；隱瞞
6.	explosive	[ɪkˋsplosɪv]	爆炸物；炸藥
7.	contain	[kənˋten]	包含；容納；控制，遏制
8.	declare	[dɪˋklɛr]	宣布，宣告；聲明
9.	separate	[ˋsɛpəˏret]	分隔；分割；使分離；使分散

🔖 Who needs to read the notice?

🔖 What things have the potential of being used to conceal explosives devices?

🔖 What do people need to do if their hand luggage have electric or electronic devices?

II-7

1.	flush	[flʌʃ]	用水沖洗；使（臉等）漲紅；使發亮
2.	sanitary	[ˋsænəˏtɛrɪ]	公共衛生的；衛生上的；衛生的；清潔的
3.	support	[səˋport]	支撐，扶持；支持，擁護，贊成；資助
4.	detect	[dɪˋtɛkt]	發現，察覺；查出，看穿
5.	assume	[əˋsjum]	以為；假定為；（想當然地）認為；承擔
6.	matter	[ˋmætɚ]	（常用於否定句和疑問句）有關係，要緊
7.	smelly	[ˋsmɛlɪ]	有強烈氣味的；臭的
8.	faulty	[ˋfɔltɪ]	有缺點的；不完美的

9.	flush away	沖洗掉
10.	flush handle	沖水扳手
11.	on fire	著火，失火；（感情，憤怒等）如火燃燒
12.	break down	撞倒；（因機械、電力等故障）停止運轉，失靈，失效；失敗；崩潰；瓦解

What can't people flush away?

Why can't people practice on the flush handle?

How do people do with the toilet?

What will happen if people smoke in the toilet?

II-8

CLEANBIQ
Disposal of Sanitary pads Only

Foot press onto pedal of the bin to open cover

1.	disposal	[dɪ`spoz!]	處理，處置；配置；布置；排列
2.	press	[prɛs]	按，壓，擠；壓碎，壓破；榨出
3.	pedal	[`pɛd!]	踏板；腳蹬；管風琴的腳踏鍵
4.	bin	[bɪn]	（貯藏穀物等的）箱子，容器，倉
5.	cover	[`kʌvɚ]	遮蓋物；蓋子；套子；（書的）封面
6.	sanitary pad		衛生棉，衛生巾，衛生墊

📌 What thing can be disposed of in the bin?

📌 How do people open the bin?

II-9

AUTOMATIC HAND DRYER
Place hands under the blower to activate

1.	automatic	[ˌɔtə`mætɪk]	自動的，自動裝置的；習慣性的
2.	blower	[`bloɚ]	吹製工；吹風機，風箱
3.	activate	[`æktəˌvet]	使活動起來；使活潑；【化】使活化
4.	hand dryer		乾手器

📌 What kind of hand dryer is it?

📌 Where do people put their hands if they want to dry their hands?

II-10

Toilet Seat
Sanitizer

PRESS

1.	sanitizer	[`sænəˌtaɪzɚ]	衛生洗滌劑；消毒殺菌劑
2.	press	[prɛs]	按，壓，擠；壓碎
3.	toilet seat		馬桶座圈

What is the sanitizer for?

How do people use the sanitizer?

II-11

1.	aluminium	[ˌæljəˈmɪnɪəm]	=aluminum 鋁
2.	glass	[glæs]	玻璃；玻璃製品

 What are the recycling items?

II-12

NO PETS
ARE ALLOWED

| 1. | pet | [pɛt] | 供玩賞的動物，寵物；寵兒；寶貝 |

📌 When seeing the sign, what can't people do?

📌 What are the three kinds of pets showed in the sign?

II-13

Please do not climb,
Walk or ride on the
conveyor belt
**THIS AREA IS UNDER
CCTV MONITORING**

1.	warning	[`wɔrnɪŋ]	警告；告誡；警報
2.	climb	[klaɪm]	爬，攀登；（植物）沿著…攀緣而上
3.	ride	[raɪd]	騎馬，乘車；乘坐，搭坐
4.	conveyor	[kən`veɚ]	搬運者；運輸裝置；傳送帶；輸送帶
5.	belt	[bɛlt]	腰帶；皮帶；帶狀物；傳送帶；傳動帶
6.	monitor	[`mɑnətɚ]	監控；監聽；監測；監視
7.	conveyor belt		傳送帶，傳遞帶
8.	conveyor belt sushi		迴轉壽司
9.	CCTV=Closed Circuit Television		閉路電視

📌 What actions are not allowed on the conveyor belt?

📌 Who is monitoring this area?

II-14

1.	handrail	[`hænd,rel]	欄杆;扶手
2.	supervise	[`supɚˌvaɪz]	監督;管理;指導
3.	lift	[lɪft]	電梯
4.	provide	[prə`vaɪd]	提供;裝備,供給

Who does the warning give to?

What do people need to do while taking the escalator?

Who needs to be supervised?

Where should people stand?

Who are suggested taking a lift?

II-15

CAUTION
RISK OF
ELECTRIC SHOCK

1.	risk	[rɪsk]	危險，風險
2.	electric	[ɪˋlɛktrɪk]	電的；導電的；發電的
3.	shock	[ʃɑk]	衝擊；震動；震驚；引起震驚的事件；打擊
4.	electric shock		電休克；觸電

Why do people need to be cautious when seeing this sign?

II-16

PRIORITY SEATS

1.	priority	[praɪˋɔrətɪ]	（時間等方面的）在先，居前；優先，重點；優先權；先取權
2.	priority seat	博愛座；敬老席	

 Who can take the priority seats based on the sign?

II-17

CHILDREN ARE NOT ALLOWED TO SEAT NEAR THE RAIL WITHOUT ADULT'S SUPERVISION.

THE MANAGENT WILL NOT BE HELD RESPONSIBLE
SHOULD ANY INCIDENT HAPPEN

1.	rail	[rel]	欄杆，扶手；圍欄；（門等的）橫木
2.	supervision	[ˌsupəˈvɪʒən]	管理；監督
3.	incident	[ˈɪnsədnt]	事件；事變；插曲

📌 Where aren't children allowed to sit if they have no adult's supervision?

📌 Who will take the responsibility if any incidents happen?

II-18

IN CASE OF FIRE

CALL AIRPORT FIRE AND
RESCUE SERVICE /
AIRPORT OPERATION CENTRE
TEL: 87768953 / 87769106

1.	rescue	[ˋrɛskju]	援救;營救;挽救
2.	operation	[ˌɑpəˋreʃən]	操作;運轉;經營;營運
3.	in case of		假使,萬一,如果發生
4.	in case of fire		萬一有火災

In case of fire, who do people call?

II-19

1.	fire alarm	火警報警器

When do people need to use the fire alarm?

Why do people need to press hard?

II-20

📌 What does the sign mean?

II-21

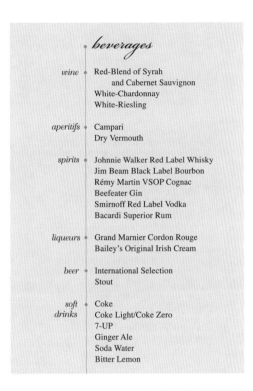

beverages

wine	Red-Blend of Syrah and Cabernet Sauvignon White-Chardonnay White-Riesling
aperitifs	Campari Dry Vermouth
spirits	Johnnie Walker Red Label Whisky Jim Beam Black Label Bourbon Rémy Martin VSOP Cognac Beefeater Gin Smirnoff Red Label Vodka Bacardi Superior Rum
liqueurs	Grand Marnier Cordon Rouge Bailey's Original Irish Cream
beer	International Selection Stout
soft drinks	Coke Coke Light/Coke Zero 7-UP Ginger Ale Soda Water Bitter Lemon

1.	beverage	[ˋbɛvərɪdʒ]	飲料
2.	aperitif	[ɑperiˋtif]	【法】開胃酒
3.	spirit	[ˋspɪrɪt]	烈酒
4.	liqueur	[lɪˋkɝ]	利口酒（具甜味而芳香的烈酒）

What do beverages contain?

What kind of beverage is Beefeater Gin?

Based on the menu, what kind of beverage would you like to request?

II-22

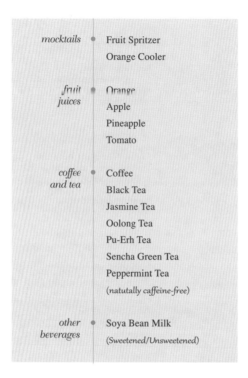

mocktails	Fruit Spritzer
	Orange Cooler
fruit juices	Orange
	Apple
	Pineapple
	Tomato
coffee and tea	Coffee
	Black Tea
	Jasmine Tea
	Oolong Tea
	Pu-Erh Tea
	Sencha Green Tea
	Peppermint Tea
	(natutally caffeine-free)
other beverages	Soya Bean Milk
	(Sweetened/Unsweetened)

1.	mocktail	[ˈmɒkteɪl]	無酒精的雞尾酒飲料
2.	jasmine	[ˈdʒæsmɪn]	茉莉；茉莉花茶
3.	peppermint	[ˈpɛpɚˌmɪnt]	薄荷，薄荷油；薄荷糖
4.	soya	[ˈsɔɪə]	=soybean 大豆
5.	soya bean milk	豆漿	

🔖 What is the difference between cocktail and mocktail?

🔖 What kinds of tea are there in the menu?

🔖 What kind of fruit juice do passengers have?

II-23

breakfast

Fruit	**Seasonal Fresh Fruit**
Main Course	**Fried Egg Noodles**
	With shredded char siew, prawns and mushrooms
	Herb Omelette
	With pan fried chicken sausage, marinated tomato and roasted potatoes
From The Bakery	**Bread Roll and Spread**
Hot Beverages	**Coffee and Tea**
	Chinese Tea

1.	main course	[men kors]	主菜
2.	shred	[ʃrɛd]	切成條狀；切絲；用碎紙機撕毀（文件）
3.	prawn	[prɔn]	明蝦；蝦
4.	omelette	[`ɑmlɪt]	煎蛋；煎蛋捲
5.	sausage	[`sɔsɪdʒ]	香腸，臘腸
6.	marinate	[`mærəˌnet]	把…浸泡在滷汁中；醃泡
7.	bakery	[`bekərɪ]	麵包（糕點）烘房；麵包（糕點）店；烘烤食品（麵包、糕點等的總稱）
8.	spread	[sprɛd]	塗食品的果醬（或奶油）

What food do passengers have for breakfast?

What do fried egg noodles include with?

What kind of beverages will be served?

II-24

lunch

international selection

Appetiser	**Smoked Salmon Salad**
Main Course	**Pan Roasted Chicken with Mushroom Sauce**
	Served with sauteed vegetables and rosemary potatoes
Dessert	**Ice Cream**
From The Bakery	**Bread Roll and Spread**
Hot Beverage	**Coffee and Tea**

1.	appetizer	[`æpəˌtaɪzɚ]	開胃的食物，開胃小吃
2.	dessert	[dɪ`zɝt]	甜點心；餐後甜點
3.	smoked	[smokt]	燻製的；用煙處理的
4.	salmon	[`sæmən]	鮭魚
5.	sautéed	[so`te]	煎炒（或炒、煸）
6.	rosemary	[`rozmɛrɪ]	迷迭香

What food do passengers have for lunch?

What food would be served with the main course?

What dessert will be served?

II-25

lunch

oriental selection

Appetiser	**Tea Smoked Duck**
	With marinated bean curd salad
Main Course	**Deep-fried Pork**
	With honey perpper sauce, Chinese vegetable and steamed rice
Dessert	**Ice Cream**
From The Bakery	**Bread Roll and Spread**
Hot Beverage	**Chinese Tea**

1.	Oriental	[ˌorɪˋɛnt!]	（大寫）東方的；亞洲的；東方人的；東方文化的；東的，東部的
2.	bean curd	豆腐	
3.	deep-fried	油炸的	

📌 What is the difference between this menu and the previous one?

📌 What food will be served with deep-fried pork?

📌 What will go with tea smoked duck?

II-26

	Lunch
Appetiser	**Sweet chilli prawns with noodle salas** marinated sweet chilli baby prawns on a bed of glass noodle salad
Main Course	**Mutton with black pepper sauce** served with creamy mashed potato, seasoned broccol, and red peppers
	Chicken with black bean sauce served with coconut rice and seasonal vegetables
Dessert	**Coconut rice pudding** garnished with tropical fruits and coconut flakes
	Cheese and biscuits
Beverages	**Tea or Coffee**
	Chocolates

1.	chilli=chili	[`tʃɪlɪ]	紅番椒（一種墨西哥菜用的調味料）
2.	mutton	[`mʌtn]	羊肉
3.	seasoned	[`siznd]	經驗豐富的；調過味的
4.	broccoli	[`brakəlɪ]	青花菜，綠花椰
5.	garnish	[`garnɪʃ]	為增加色香味而添加的配菜；裝飾物
6.	tropical	[`trɑpɪk!]	熱帶的；位於熱帶的；酷熱的
7.	flake	[flek]	小薄片；扁薄的一層；玉米片
8.	biscuit	[`bɪskɪt]	【美】小麵包；軟餅；【英】餅乾
9.	mashed potato		馬鈴薯泥；洋芋泥

★ What do they have for the main course?

★ What kind of desserts can passengers have?

★ What food will be served with mutton?

II-27

Instant cup noodles

instant cup noodles are available on request
when meals are not being served

1.	instant	[`ɪnstənt]	立即的，即刻的；緊迫的；迫在眉睫的
2.	request	[rɪ`kwɛst]	要求，請求
3.	instant noodles	泡麵	

If passengers are hungry but meals are not being served, what can they do?

II-28

Savoury Snack

Honey mustard chicken
Wholemeal panini bread roll filled with honey mustard flavoured chicken and coleslaw salad

Chocolate muffin

Tea or Coffee

1.	savoury	[`sevərɪ]	可口的；味香的；鹹味的；舒適的
2.	snack	[snæk]	快餐；小吃，點心
3.	mustard	[`mʌstəd]	芥末
4.	wholemeal	[`holmil]	全麥麵粉；全（小）麥
5.	panini	[pəˈniːni]	義式麵包做成的三明治
6.	coleslaw	[`kol͵slɔ]	【美】涼拌卷心菜
7.	muffin	[`mʌfɪn]	鬆餅
8.	bread roll	小麵包；麵包捲	

What is the menu about?

What kind of snacks can passengers have?

What will be filled with honey mustard flavored chicken and coleslaw salad?

II-29

MENU

PASSION FRUIT AND SCENTED PUMPKIN [1]
MEDITERRANEAN SALAD [2]

please choose from our selection :

SAUTÉED BEEF WITH GARLIC OYSTER SAUCE [3]
mixed vegetables / steamed rice

or

PENNE [4]
creamy pesto sauce
seasonal vegetables

————

HONEY CAKE [5]

before landing

YOGHURT [6]
ASSORTED CHEESE [7]

1.	scented	[`sɛntɪd]	散發香味的；芳香的
2.	pumpkin	[`pʌmpkɪn]	南瓜
3.	Mediterranean	[ˌmɛdətə`renɪən]	地中海的；地中海沿岸地區的
4.	oyster	[`ɔɪstɚ]	牡蠣；蠔
5.	penne	[`pɛneɪ]	管狀義大利麵食
6.	assorted	[ə`sɔrtɪd]	各色具備的，什錦的；各種各樣（混在一起）的
7.	passion fruit		百香果

📌 What are the main courses?

📌 What kind of dessert will be served?

📌 What will be served before landing?

II-30

please choose from our selection :
RICE NOODLES [1]
CHICKEN MINCED SAUCE [9]
local vegetables

or

SCRAMBLED EGGS [10]
sautéed mushrooms / roasted tomatoes

butter / jam [11]
ovenfresh bread selection [12]

1.	mince	[mɪns]	切碎，剁碎；絞碎
2.	jam	[dʒæm]	果醬
3.	rice noodles	米線，米粉	
4.	scrambled eggs	炒蛋	
5.	ovenfresh	新鮮出爐	

What food will go with scrambled eggs?

What will go with bread?

II-31

hot snack

to commence
oriental coleslaw salad

to follow
braised beef in black pepper
stir fried egg noodle with carrots and celery

grilled chicked with tarragon sauce
fried potato, steamed broccoli and carrots

sweet finale
baked honey cheese cake

sofe roll

1.	commence	[kə`mɛns]	開始;著手
2.	braise	[brez]	以文火燉煮
3.	stir-fry	[`stɝˌfraɪ]	炒
4.	celery	[`sɛlərɪ]	芹菜
5.	grilled	[grɪld]	烤的;炙過的;有格子的
6.	tarragon	[`tærəˌgən]	龍蒿
7.	finale	[fɪ`nɑlɪ]	結局,終了,最後的一個樂章,終曲

📌 To start with, what can passengers have?

📌 What main dish can passengers choose?

📌 What snack will go after the main dish?

II-32

breakfast

to commence
selection of seasonal fresh fruits

to follow
mushroom and onion omelette
roasted potatoes, green beans and tomato

congee
shrimp, mushroom and asparagus

croissant

Please accept our apologies if your first choice is not available
This meal is prepared according to Islamic principles

1.	onion	[`ʌnjən]	洋蔥
2.	congee	[`kɑndʒi]	傳統中國式的白米粥
3.	asparagus	[ə`spærəgəs]	蘆筍
4.	croissant	[krwɑ`sɑn]	牛角麵包，可頌
5.	apology	[ə`pɑlədʒɪ]	道歉；陪罪
6.	Islamic	[ɪs`læmɪk]	伊斯蘭的；伊斯蘭教徒的
7.	principle	[`prɪnsəp!]	原則；原理
8.	according to		根據，按照

What can passengers have for breakfast at the beginning?

What food is served for breakfast?

What is the meal prepared according to?

II-33

beverages

complimentary
hot and cold
beverages are
available throughout
the flight

Wines
champagne
red wines
white wines

spirits
scotch whisky
gin
vodka
brandy

beer
heineken
foster's lager

1.	complimentary	[ˌkɑmpləˋmɛntərɪ]	贈送的；讚賞的；恭維的
2.	throughout	[θruˋaʊt]	遍及，遍布；貫穿，從頭到尾

How much do passengers pay for the beverages served throughout the flight?

What kind of spirits are there?

What kind of beverages are there in the menu?

II-34

non-alcoholic
orange juice
apple juice
tomato juice
pineapple juice
mineral water
soda water
tonic water
ginger ale
sprite
diet sprite
coca cola
diet coca cola
fanta orange

tea or coffee

*should you require
any assistance,
please do not
hesitate to ask
your flight attendant*

1.	alcoholic	[͵ælkə`hɔlɪk]	酒精的；含酒精的；由酒精引起的
2.	require	[rɪ`kwaɪr]	需要
3.	hesitate	[`hɛzə͵tet]	躊躇；猶豫
4.	mineral water		礦泉水
5.	tonic water		奎寧水，開胃水（一種加有奎寧的汽水飲料）
6.	ginger ale		薑味較淡的薑汁汽水
7.	flight attendant		空中服務人員

How many non-alcoholic beverages are listed in the menu?

In addition to non-alcoholic beverages, what else are there?

Who can passengers ask for help?

II-35

Starter
Fresh fruit

Main Courses
Braised chicken with garlic in soya sauce
Steamed rice

or

Pan-seared assorted seafood with caper tomato sauce
Tri-colour fusilli pasta, asparagus and cherry tomato

Bread Selection

Tea and Coffee

1.	starter	[`stɑrtɚ]	開胃菜；第一道菜
2.	sear	[sɪr]	燒烤；打烙印
3.	caper	[`kepɚ]	【植】續隨子，馬檳榔，刺山柑
4.	fusilli		螺旋麵（義大利麵的一種）
5.	cherry tomato		小番茄

🖈 What can passengers have for the starter?

🖈 What are the main courses?

🖈 What is steamed rice served with?

🖈 What is fusilli pasta served with?

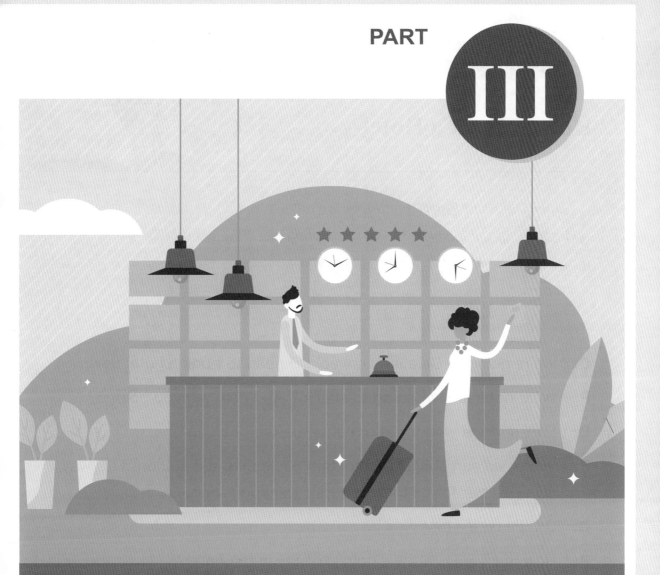

III

Accommodation & Meals
訂房及餐飲

Lesson 7

How to Book a Hotel

Ding-Ding and Ping-Ping are going to visit a client in Oslo, Norway. After taking care of the business, Ding-Ding and Ping-Ping would like to stay in that city for three days and travel around.

D: We're going to Oslo in two weeks. I need to book a hotel now.

P: What hotel are we going to stay in? And how will you book it?

D: I will surf the web for information before booking one.

P: I think we can stay in a hotel that is close to the station. This way, it'll be easier for us to take public transportation.

D: OK, I'll take a look.

P: How many days are we going to stay in the hotel?

D: We should arrive in Oslo in the early morning, around 6:00. Then we are visiting the client around 11:00. I made an appointment with him by e-mail a week ago. He said that he can give us a ride.

P: After the 11:00am meeting, we have 2.5 more days to explore.

D: Well, it's a good chance to travel around a new city. After the business part, we can start touring in the afternoon.

P: It's great. So, how about that hotel you were looking for?

D: I've found one near the subway station. It includes breakfast. They have an en suite double bed. And, the price rate is reasonable compared to other hotels nearby.

P: Not bad. We can stay there for three days, so we'll book for two nights, right?

D: Yes. Now, I have to pay for the room by credit card.

P: What time is check-in?

D: It's at noon.

P: Then what do we do with our luggage?

D: I'll see if we can check in our room earlier. If not, we can leave our luggage in their storage room. Usually, hotels offer this kind of service.

P: Hopefully. I don't want to be carrying a heavy bag walking around a big city.

D: Take it easy. We'll be fine.

I. Vocabulary words and phrases

1.	client	[`klaɪənt]	客戶
2.	book	[bʊk]	預訂
3.	storage	[`storɪdʒ]	貯藏庫
4.	surf the web	瀏覽網頁	
5.	public transportation	公共運輸	
6.	make an appointment	預約	
7.	en suite double bed	套房式雙人房	
8.	price rate	價格	

II. Answering the following questions

1. Why do Ding-Ding and Ping-Ping go to Oslo?

2. How do they book their hotel?

3. How do they plan to deal with their luggage before check-in time?

Check-in at the Hotel

After disembarking from the plane, Ding-Ding and Ping-Ping go to the baggage claim area to pick up their luggage. Then, they take the airport rail link directly to the hotel.

D: Can you keep an eye on the luggage? I need to go to the restroom.

P: Sure. Take your time. There aren't many passengers at this time.

A few minutes later, Ding-Ding comes back.

D: OK, now, let's see how to get to the airport rail link station.

P: There's a sign there, just down the hall.

D: Here we are. I'll buy the tickets.

P: We can buy them at the ticket vending machine. It's very convenient.

After getting off the train and getting out of the station, they are trying to figure out how to get to the hotel with Google Maps.

D: It says that it takes fifteen minutes to get there on foot.

P: Great. Now, you'll be the navigator and lead us to our destination.

They are arriving at the hotel now.

Hotel receptionist: Good morning. May I help you?

D: Good morning. I've booked a room for two on the internet. I'd like to know if we can check in now.

Hotel receptionist: May I have your name please?

Ding-Ding shows the receptionist his passport.

Hotel receptionist: OK, sir. The room is being cleaned and is not available now. Check-in starts at 3:00 in the afternoon.

D: May I leave my luggage here until then?

Hotel receptionist: Yes, we have a luggage storage room where you can store your luggage.

D: That's great. Thank you very much.

Ding-Ding and Ping-Ping leave their luggage at the hotel and go to visit their client. A few hours later, they return to the hotel.

D: Hi, I'd like to check in now and get my luggage.

The hotel receptionist goes to get the luggage and comes back to the front desk.

Hotel receptionist: Here's your room card and you have free breakfast. The restaurant is in the basement. Breakfast opening hours are from 7:00am to 10:00am.

D: Thank you very much. Where's the elevator?

Hotel receptionist: Just walk down the corridor and turn left. Have a pleasant stay.

I. Vocabulary words and phrases

1.	disembark	[ˌdɪsɪmˋbɑrk]	登陸
2.	navigator	[ˋnævəˌgetɚ]	領航員
3.	receptionist	[rɪˋsɛpʃənɪst]	接待員
4.	then	[ðɛn]	那時
5.	store	[stor]	保管
6.	corridor	[ˋkɔrɪdɚ]	走廊
7.	vending machine		自動販賣機
8.	figure out		理解
9.	on foot		步行
10.	front desk		櫃檯
11.	opening hours		營業時間

II. Answering the following questions

1. How do they get their tickets for the airport rail link?

2. How do they get to the hotel?

3. When are the opening hours for breakfast?

Lesson 9

In the Restaurant

When Ding-Ding and Ping-Ping finish visiting, they wanted to thank people who help take care of students doing internships.

P: I'd like to treat Mary and Clair to lunch for their kind help.

D: We need to check when they are available.

P: I already have. They said that they are free for brunch on Saturday. Also, I invited Clair's husband to join us. They have given me a lot of help since I did the overseas internship project.

D: I agree. Do we need to make a reservation in advance?

P: I already have.

It is Saturday morning. Ding-Ding and Ping-Ping are ready to go to the restaurant. Mary arrives to give them a ride.

P: Good morning, Mary. Thank you for the ride.

Mary: No problem. So, everything's ready?

P: Yes.

When they arrive at the restaurant, Clair and her husband are already waiting for them.

Clair: Hello and good morning!

P: Good morning. Looks like we're all here. Shall we go in?

They enter the restaurant and wait to be seated. Soon, a waitress comes over.

Waitress: How many people?

D: Five. We have a reservation.

Waitress: Please follow me. Here's your table and menu.

D: Thanks.

> *The waitress gives everyone a glass of water and leaves.*

D: OK. Let's see what's on the menu.

Mary: I've heard that the omelets are very famous here. You should try one.

D: Thanks for the recommendation. I think I will.

Later on, the waitress comes back.

Waitress: Are you ready to order?

Mary: Yes, may I have a burrito?

Waitress: What would you like to drink?

Mary: Water is fine. Thanks.

Everyone is enjoying a pleasant chat. A few hours later, they finish their meal and the waitress gives them the check. In addition to the meal, Ding-Ding gives a tip for the service.

I. Vocabulary words and phrases

1.	treat	[trit]	款待
2.	overseas	[ˋovɚˋsiz]	在（或向）海外
3.	omelet	[ˋɑmlɪt]	煎蛋餅
4.	recommendation	[͵rɛkəmɛnˋdeʃən]	推薦
5.	burrito	[bɝˋrɪto]	玉米粉捲餅
6.	tip	[tɪp]	小費
7.	make a reservation	預定	
8.	in advance	預先	
9.	to be seated	請坐	
10.	in addition to	除了 ... 尚有	

II. Answering the following questions

1. Why do Ding-Ding and Ping-Ping want to treat their friends to a meal?

2. What do people usually do if they want to make sure they have a table at the restaurant?

3. In addition to paying for the meal, what do customers do for the waiter/ waitress in the U.S.?

Practice

III-1

PLEASE
RING THE BELL
AT THE "FRONT" DOOR
FOR ATTENTION

1.	ring	[rɪŋ]	按（鈴）；搖（鈴）；敲（鐘）；打電話給…
2.	bell	[bɛl]	鐘；鈴；門鈴；鐘聲；鈴聲
3.	attention	[ə`tɛnʃən]	注意；注意力；專心

📌 Where do people ring the bell?

📌 Why do people ring the bell?

III-2

GUESTS MAY USE THIS ROOM TO WATCH TV OR FOR READING FROM 10am UNTIL 10pm

| 1. | guest | [gɛst] | 客人，賓客；旅客；顧客 |

What can guests do in the room?

What time can they use the room?

III-3

PRESS THIS BUTTON TO OPEN DOOR

| 1. | press | [prɛs] | 按，壓，擠；壓碎，壓破；榨出 |
| 2. | button | [ˋbʌtn] | 按鈕；鈕扣，釦子 |

📌 When people want to open the door, what do they need to do?

III-4

NOTICE

KEEP DOOR CLOSED AT ALL TIMES

| 1. | notice | [`notɪs] | 公告，通知，貼示 |
| 2. | at all times | 隨時，永遠 | |

When do people keep door closed?

III-5

PLEASE MAKE UP ROOM

| 1. | make up room | 打掃房間 |

What does the sign mean?

Where is the sign usually used?

 III-6

1.	disturb	[dɪsˋtɝb]	打擾，妨礙

What does the sign mean?

Where is the sign used?

III-7

1.	suite	[swit]	套房
2.	lane	[len]	小路；巷，弄；車道，線道
3.	view	[vju]	景色；視力；視野；觀看；眺望
4.	vacancy	[ˋvekənsɪ]	空；空白；空間；空處；空地；空房
5.	cottage	[ˋkɑtɪdʒ]	農舍，小屋

📌 What is Bed & Breakfast abbreviated?

📌 What is the name of the B & B?

📌 What kind of bedrooms does it provide?

★ What does Willowbank look like?

★ How special is it?

★ What does No Vacancies mean?

III-8

1.	upstairs	[`ʌp`stɛrz]	樓上；在樓上的；在樓上；往樓上
2.	check in		到達並登記；報到；記錄
3.	check out		辦理退房手續；結帳離開；檢查；合格，通過

📌 When is the check-in time?

📌 When is the check-out time on Sundays?

III-9

LUGGAGE?

You can feel free to leave your luggage
with us, but we are not responsible for
any of your personal belongings.

COMFORT HOTEL®
FOR URBAN EASY LIVING

1.	feel free	（用以表示准許）請隨意，請便
2.	be responsible for	對…負責，負責…；是…的起因
3.	personal belongings	個人的行李，個人的所有物

🔖 Who can guests leave their luggage with?

🔖 Who is responsible for personal belongings?

III-10

1.	trouser	[ˋtraʊzɚ]	（常複數）褲子；長褲	
2.	donate	[ˋdonet]	捐獻，捐贈	
3.	sustainable	[səˋstenəb!]	支撐得住的；能承受的；能維持的	
4.	charity	[ˋtʃærətɪ]	慈悲，仁愛，博愛；慈善；施捨；善舉	
5.	fortunate	[ˋfɔrtʃənɪt]	幸運的，僥倖的	
6.	make a difference		有影響，有關係	
7.	tired of		厭煩	

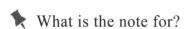 Who is the note given to?

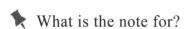 What is the note for?

III-11

DRINK MORE WATER

Our tap water is free, clean and drinkable

1.	drinkable	[`drɪŋkəb!]	可以喝的；（常用複）飲料
2.	tap water		自來水（非蒸餾水）

What is the sign for?

What features does the tap water have?

III-12

GO EASY
ON THE
PLANET

Use your towel more than once

1.	planet	[`plænɪt]	行星
2.	towel	[`taʊəl]	毛巾，手巾；紙巾；用毛巾擦
3.	go easy on		寬容溫和地對待（某人）；節約，節省

What is the sign for?

III-13

1.	recycle	[ri`saɪk!]	使再循環；再利用
2.	throw	[θro]	投，擲，拋，扔
3.	bin	[bɪn]	垃圾箱；（貯藏穀物等的）箱子，容器，倉

📌 What things cannot throw in the bin?

III-14

HAND WASH

Softly cleans your hands
without drying them out.

VEGAN INGREDIENTS
INFUSED WITH A FRESH FRAGRANCE

1.	vegan	[`vɛgən]	嚴守素食主義的人；嚴守素食主義的
2.	ingredient	[ɪnˋgridɪənt]	（混合物的）組成部分；（烹調的）原料；（構成）要素，因素
3.	infuse	[ɪnˋfjuz]	將…注入；（向…）灌輸（+into）；使充滿；鼓舞（+with）
4.	fragrance	[`fregrəns]	芬芳；香味；香氣
5.	hand wash		洗手液
6.	dry out		漸漸失去水分而變乾

What features does the hand wash have?

What kind of ingredients does the hand wash have?

III-15

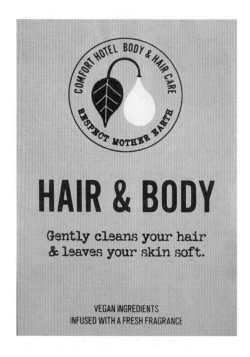

COMFORT HOTEL BODY & HAIR CARE
RESPECT MOTHER EARTH

HAIR & BODY

Gently cleans your hair
& leaves your skin soft.

VEGAN INGREDIENTS
INFUSED WITH A FRESH FRAGRANCE

| 1. | gently | [`dʒɛntlɪ] | 溫柔地;溫和地;輕輕地;和緩地;小心地 |

What does the sign mean?

III-16

Public Restroom
Please proceed to the lower deck of
Hornbill Restaurant

1.	proceed	[prə`sid]	（沿特定路線）行進；開始，著手，出發
2.	deck	[dɛk]	（船的）艙面，甲板
3.	public restroom	公共廁所	
4.	lower deck	下層甲板	

📌 Where does the arrow point to?

📌 Where is the public restroom?

III-17

Vær varsom!
Caution!

Taket har mange avsatser, og
kan være glatt. Bruk av sykkel
eller skateboard er forbudt.
Ferdsel på eget ansvar.

The roof has many steps, and
may be slippery. Bicycles or
skateboards not allowed. Use
of the area is at your own risk.

1.	roof	[ruf]	屋頂；車頂；住屋，家
2.	slippery	[`slɪpərɪ]	滑的；（問題等）須小心對待的
3.	skateboard	[`sket͵bord]	滑板
4.	at one's own risk		自擔風險（同意不要求賠償損失、損害等）

What does the roof have?

How are those steps?

What activities are not allowed to do there?

Who will take the responsibility, if someone plays skateboard games and gets hurt?

III-18

| 1. | seat | [sit] | 使就座;有…座位;座位 |

Where can people see the sign?

What do people do when they see the sign?

III-19

Singles	
Soft Taco	2.20
Fajita Taco	2.99
Quesadilla	1.99
Chicken or Beef Fajita Quesadilla	2.99
Enchilada	1.25
Chalupa	1.25
Crispy Taco	1.25
Tortilla	.40
Guacamole	1.99
Chile Relleno	2.25
Queso	
Small	1.99
Large	3.49
Rice or Beans	.99
Gorditas	2.25

Beverages	
Coke, Diet Coke, Dr. Pepper, & Sprite	1.75
Tea	1.40
To-Go Tea	1.69
Coffee	.99
Milk	1.75
Orange Juice	1.80

Call in orders welcomed
Party of 6 or more require a 15% gratuity charge
Thank you, please call again!

1.	taco	[`tɑko]	墨西哥煎玉米捲
2.	gratuity	[grə`tjuətɪ]	賞錢,小費
3.	charge	[tʃɑrdʒ]	費用,價錢,索價

📌 How much does it cost if the customer orders fajita taco and chalupa?

📌 How much is it for the to-go tea?

📌 What do customers need to do if they have a party of 8 persons?

III-20

American Food

all dinners are served with french fries or mashed potatoes, texas toast & gravy

Ribeye Steak 10.99

served with french fries, salad & texas toast

Small Chicken Fried Steak 6.99
Large Chicken Fried Steak 7.99
Chicken Strip Dinner 7.99
Steak Finger Dinner 6.49
Hamburger Steak 7.99
Hamburgers
   Regular Hamburger 3.20
   Cheeseburger 3.69
   Double Meat Cheeseburger 4.59

1.	gravy	[ˋgrevɪ]	肉汁；（作調味用的）滷
2.	chicken fried steak	炸牛排肉	
3.	chicken strip	雞肉條	
4.	steak finger	條狀牛排	

What kind of food is on the menu?

What kinds of hamburgers does it serve?

What will be served with dinner?

III-21

Salads

Guacamole Salad	4.99
Taco Salad	4.99
Green Salad	2.99
Chef Salad	5.49
With Chicken Strips	6.49
Fajita Salad	7.99
beef or chicken with guacamole	

Salad Dressings: Ranch, Thousand Island, French

1.	guacamole	[gwɑkə`molɪ]	酪梨醬
2.	dressing	[`drɛsɪŋ]	（拌沙拉等用的）調料
3.	fajita		墨西哥烤肉

What meal is on the menu?

What will be served if the customer orders chef salad?

What kind of salad dressings are there?

III-22

Mexican Food

All Mexican Plates served with Rice, Refried Beans, & Salad

Chicken Fajita Dinner 8.99	
includes pico de gallo, guacamole, & 2 tortillas	
Beef Fajita Dinner 8.99	
includes pico de gallo, guacamole, & 2 tortillas	
Mexican Dinner 6.99	
2 enchiladas, 2 crispy tacos, salad not included	
Chalupa Dinner 6.99	
salad not included	
Quesadilla Dinner	
2 flour tortillas folded & grilled with cheese,	
includes pico de gllo & guacamole	
Beef, Chicken or Cheese 6.99	

1.	plate	[plet]	盤子，盆，碟；一盤食物
2.	tortilla	[tɔr`tijɑ]	（墨西哥）玉米粉薄烙餅
3.	crispy	[`krɪspɪ]	酥脆的；清脆的；涼爽的
4.	refried beans		豆泥

📌 What kind of food is on the menu?

📌 What will be served with Mexican plates?

📌 What will be included for beef fajita dinner?

III-23

20 WEST BEAUREGARD
SAN ANGELO, TX 76901
325.653.5123

WWW.FACEBOOK.

APPETIZERS

CRISPY DUCK WINGS
Tossed with a sweet green curry glaze...$9

BUFFALO WINGS
Tossed in our house wing sauce, served with gorgonzola
dipping sauce...$7.5

BBQ PORK NACHOS
Pulled pork, cheddar cheese, house BBQ, black beans,
guacamole, creme fraiche and salsa...$10

CHIPOTLE REMOULADE CRAB CAKE
Super lump crab cake, chipotle remoulade served with
small mixed green salad with balsamic dressing...$9

PORTABELLA MUSHROOM
Stuffed with spinach, artichoke and gorgonzola. Served
with small mixed green salad with balsamic dressing ...$10

HOP SALTED FRIED CALAMARI
Served with a house-crafted IPA sweet thai chili
sauce...$8.5

WEST TEXAS WHITE QUESO
Served with tortilla chips...$9

SALADS

HOUSE SPECIAL

PAN SEARED TERIYAKI
Served with your choice of

GUAPOTLE PULLED PO
Pulled pork, guapotle sauc
house made queso fresco,
tortillas served with black

BLACKENED FISH TA
Blackened fish, purple ca
made queso fresco,flour
with black bean pilaf...$

BEER TEMPURA BA
Served with tartar sauc

THAI RED CURRY
Chicken, snow peas, b
mushrooms, in a spic
on sticky rice...$11
Substitute Tofu...$10

SAUSAGE TRIO
Bratwurst, andouille
warm mustard-bas

SEARED TUNA

1.	appetizer	[ˋæpəˌtaɪzɚ]	開胃的食物;開胃小吃
2.	crispy	[ˋkrɪspɪ]	酥脆的;清脆的;涼爽的
3.	buffalo	[ˋbʌfəlou]	水牛;(北美)野牛;(大寫)(美國紐約州城市)水牛城
4.	wing	[wɪŋ]	翅膀;機翼;【建】側廳,廂房
5.	nachos	[ˋnætʃoz]	(墨西哥人食用的)烤乾酪辣味玉米片
6.	remoulade	[ˌremuˋlad]	加料的蛋黃醬
7.	mushroom	[ˋmʌʃrʊm]	蘑菇;傘菌;蕈;蘑菇形物
8.	artichoke	[ˋɑrtɪˌtʃok]	【植】朝鮮薊(形似百合果的綠果)
9.	calamari	[ˋkæləˌmɛrɪ]	=calamari 槍烏賊

What's the name of the restaurant?

Which appetizer will be served with gorgonzola dipping sauce?

What will Portabella mushroom be stuffed with?

If customers order west Texas white queso, what thing will be served?

III-24

 WWW.FACEBOOK.COM/**ZERO**ONE**ALE**HOUSE

HOUSE SPECIALITIES

PAN SEARED TERIYAKI SALMON
Served with your choice of two sides...$19

GUAPOTLE PULLED PORK TACOS
Pulled pork, guapotle sauce, purple cabbage slaw, cilantro,
house made queso fresco, pickled red onions, flour or corn
tortillas served with black bean pilaf...$10

BLACKENED FISH TACOS
Blackened fish, purple cabbage slaw, mango pico, house
made queso fresco, flour or corn tortillas served
with black bean pilaf...$14

BEER TEMPURA BATTERED FISH AND CHIPS
Served with tartar sauce...$13

THAI RED CURRY
Chicken, snow peas, broccoli, red bell pepper, shiitake
mushrooms, in a spicy coconut milk red curry sauce
on sticky rice...$11
Substitute Tofu...$10 Subsitute Shrimp...$14 Add Shrimp...$16

SAUSAGE TRIO
Bratwurst, andouille and jalapeño sausage served over a
warm mustard-based German potato salad...$15

SEARED TUNA
Cooked to temperature with snow peas, broccoli, red bell pepp
shiitake mushrooms, sticky rice and a sweet wasabi sauce.
Served with Japanese marinated cucumbers...$13

SPICY HERB ROASTED CHICKEN
Half chicken, twice baked fried potato balls and
vegetable of the day...$15

1.	pan	[pæn]	平底鍋
2.	sear	[sɪr]	燒烤;打烙印
3.	teriyaki	[ˌtɛrɪˋjɑkɪ]	串烤魚貝(一道日本料理)
4.	salmon	[ˋsæmən]	鮭魚
5.	taco	[ˋtɑko]	炸玉米餅(或捲)
6.	tempura	[ˋtɛmpʊrə]	天婦羅(一種由蔬菜和蝦,海產搗泥炸成之日本料理)
7.	batter	[ˋbætɚ]	用雞蛋,牛奶,麵粉等調成的)糊狀物
8.	curry	[ˋkɝɪ]	咖喱;咖喱粉
9.	sausage	[ˋsɔsɪdʒ]	香腸,臘腸
10.	trio	[ˋtrio]	三個(或三人)一組;三件一套;三重唱(或三重奏)的樂曲

11.	tuna	[`tunə]	鮪，金鎗魚
12.	spicy	[`spaɪsɪ]	香的，多香料的，辛辣的
13.	herb	[ɝb hɝb]	草本植物；芳草；藥草
14.	roast	[rost]	烤；烤肉；烘烤的

Which speciality will be served with tartar sauce?

What ingredients does Thai Red Curry include?

Which speciality will be served with Japanese marinated cucumbers?

What do they have for the dish of Spicy Herb Roasted Chicken?

III-25

SHEEP
HEID INN

Some thing in life really are free!

Would you like a free coffee of your
choice at the end your meal?

There are 4 simple steps to attaining this:

1. Get your smart phone out.

2. Scan the QR code at the bottom of the page or
   go to the following website www.bestvillagepubs.co.uk

3. Complete the survey-the telephone number is
   01316617974(You can even use the free Wi-Fi!)

4. Show your server the "thank you for participating"
   message and order any coffee of your choice on the house!

Simple! But remember only strongly agrees count!

1.	attain	[ə`ten]	達到；獲得；到達
2.	scan	[skæn]	細看；審視；粗略一看；瀏覽
3.	bottom	[`batəm]	底；底部；下端
4.	complete	[kəm`plit]	完成；結束；使齊全；使完整
5.	survey	[`sɜːveɪ]	調查
6.	server	[`sɜ·və·]	侍者；伺服器
7.	participating	[par`tɪsə͵pet]	參加，參與
8.	message	[`mɛsɪdʒ]	口信，信息；消息，音信，電文，通訊
9.	agree	[ə`gri]	同意，贊同
10.	count	[kaʊnt]	有重要意義，有價值

What may the customers have at the end of the meal?

Where can the customers scan the QR code?

What do the customers need to do after accessing to the website?

What message do the customers show the server?

III-26

Breakfast

JR's Breakfast Scramble
Diced Potato, Fresh Jalapeno, Ham, Onions, Tomatoes,
Scrambled Eggs topped with Shredded Cheese, Fresh Salsa
& Warm Tortillas or Toast
$6.00

Wildcatter's Breakfast
Choice of (1) Pancake, French Toast or Biscuit &
Gravy, 2 Eggs your way w/ Bacon or Sausage.
$5.75

Brisket & Chorizo Hash
Pan Fried Potatoes, Beef Brisket and Chorizo
Topped with two Eggs your way and Cheese
served with Fresh Salsa & Warm Tortillas or Toast
$7.50

New Mexico Omelet
2 Egg Omelet with Chorizo, Onions, Tomatoes, Bell
Peppers topped with Enchilada Sauce & Cheese- Served
with Fresh Salsa & warm Tortillas
$7.00

Breakfast Burrito
2 Eggs, diced Potato, Cheese, Bell Peppers, Onions,
Choice of Sausage or Bacon w/ Fresh Salsa.
$5.75

Muffin on the Run
1 Egg, cooked your way w/ Cheese on a
Toasted English Muffin
$2.25
(Add Bacon or Sausage for $2.00 More)

Baked Fresh Daily
Cinnamon Rolls, Assorted Scones & Muffins..........$2.50

1.	diced	[daɪs]	將（蔬菜等）切成小方塊
2.	burrito	[bɚˋrɪto]	玉米粉捲餅
3.	scone	[skon]	【英】烤鬆餅；司康
4.	cinnamon roll	肉桂捲	

📌 What meal is served on the menu?

📌 Which is the most expensive dish?

📌 What food will be served if the customer orders baked fresh daily?

Lunch

All Burgers & Sandwiches come garnished w/ Lettuce, Tomato, Pickles & Onions and served w/ Choice of House Chips, Steak or Spicy Fries, Onion Rings , Tots, Fruit , Potato Salad, or a small Green Salad.

Smoked Brisket Sandwich
Sliced Smoked Brisket, BBQ sauce & Pepper Jack Cheese Served open-faced on Sour Dough topped with Crispy Fried Onions & Choice of Side
$7.85

Philly Cheesesteak
½ LB Beef or Chicken, Sautéed Peppers & Onions, Provolone Cheese & Choice of Side
$7.85

The Manor Burger
¼ lb Patty w/ choice of Cheese
$6.00

Smoked Chicken Quesadilla
Smoked Chicken, Onions, Bell peppers, and Green Chilies w/ Cheddar Cheese Served with Fresh Salsa and a Side
$7.00

Patty Melt
¼ lb Patty w/ Grilled Onions, Swiss Cheese on Rye
$6.50

Grilled Club Wrap
Bacon, Turkey, Ham, wrapped in a Flour Tortilla w/ Lettuce, Tomato & Cheddar Cheese
$7.00

The Monterey
Grilled Chicken Breast, w/ Green Chili, Tomatoes, Avocado, Lettuce & Cheese
$6.50

Blackened Salmon
Served over Angel Hair Pasta w/ Tomatoes, Bell Peppers & Alfredo Sauce
$7.85

Rueben
Classic sandwich with Corned Beef, Sauerkraut, Swiss Cheese and tangy 1000 Island Dressing
$6.50

Buffalo Wings
6 or 8 Spicy wings Served with Sauce for the dipping and choice of Side
$7 / $9

1.	lettuce	[ˋlɛtɪs]	萵苣
2.	pickle	[ˋpɪk!]	醃漬食品；醃菜，泡菜
3.	tot	[tɑt]	少量；一口；一杯
4.	brisket	[ˋbrɪskɪt]	胸脯肉
5.	patty melt		【美】（放在麵包上吃的）上覆一層起司煮的牛肉片

📌 What meal is served on the menu?

📌 How much will the customer pay if they order 8 buffalo wings?

📌 Which dish is the cheapest one?

III-28

Wildcatter's Favorites

Chicken Strips or Steak Fingers w/ Texas Toast, Gravy & a side.................... $6.00
Signature Chicken Salad, in a Sandwich or over a bed of Lettuce.................$6.00
Grilled Cheese, Tomato & Avocado Sandwich w/1 side............................. $5.50
Grilled Cheese w/ 1 Side.................$4.00.(add Ham or Turkey...............$5.00
Deli Sandwich (Ham or Turkey), choice of Cheese..........................$5.00
Soup of the Day...Cup $2.00 ...Bowl..$4.00 Cup of Soup & ½ Deli Sandwich...$4.50

Beverages

Fountain Drinks & Ice Tea- **$0.95 / $1.50**
Bottled Sodas $1.75
Juices......$1.75
Bottled Water.....$1.00

Desserts

Slice of Cake or Pie $2.50

1.	avocado	[ˌævəˈkɑdo]	酪梨
2.	deli	[ˈdɛlɪ]	現成的食品；熟食店
3.	bowl	[bol]	碗
4.	slice	[slaɪs]	薄片，切片，片
5.	fountain drinks		自動飲水器的飲料
6.	signature chicken salad		招牌雞肉沙拉

What do they serve for the desserts?

How much is the cup of soup?

How will signature chicken salad be served?

How much is it for the bottled water?

III-29

Notice:

In accordance with Manor Park Policy, Tipping is not allowed. Consuming raw or undercooked meats, poultry, seafood or eggs may increase your risk of food borne illness, especially if you have certain medical conditions. Here at Manor Park, We are proud to use Pasteurized Eggs.

1.	notice	[`notɪs]	公告，通知，貼示
2.	tip	[tɪp]	給小費；；小費
3.	allow	[ə`laʊ]	允許，准許
4.	consume	[kən`sjum]	消耗，花費；耗盡；吃完，喝光
5.	raw	[rɔ]	生的；未加工的；處於自然狀態的
6.	undercook	[ˌʌndɚ`kʊk]	未煮透
7.	poultry	[`poltrɪ]	家禽
8.	risk	[rɪsk]	危險，風險
9.	pasteurize	[`pæstɚˌraɪz]	對…進行加熱殺菌
10.	borne		表示運載的，輸送的

📌 Based on Manor Park Policy, what is a customer not allowed to do?

📌 If customers are having undercooked meats or raw seafood, what will they risk?

📌 Why does Manor Park feel proud of?

Road Signs

路標

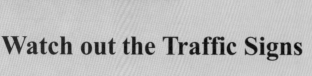

Lesson 10

Watch out the Traffic Signs

Ding-Ding and Ping-Ping's friend, Henry, was taking them to visit a university.

H: I'm going to take you guys to a university. It is famous for its beautiful campus.

D: Great. How long will it take to get there?

H: It's about a 20 minute drive if the traffic is nice.

D: I'll sit next to you. Ping-Ping, can you sit in the back?

P: Sure. Do I need to fasten the seat belt?

H: Yes, please. Now, let's go.

D: Compared to the traffic in Taiwan, there are not many cars on the road.

H: Yeah, that's because we are not in the big city and it's a college town. So, the traffic is kind of smooth and light.

D: There is a stop sign at the intersection. What do we need to do?

H: When drivers see a stop sign, they have to bring their cars to a full stop. They need to make sure the intersection is clear. If so, they can drive through.

P: Who has the right of way at a four-way stop?

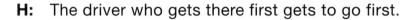

H: The driver who gets there first gets to go first.

P: That's very interesting.

H: Do you see the sign ahead? It says, "Right Lane MUST Turn Right".

P: So, drivers who intend to go straight or turn left cannot drive in the right lane, right?

H: That's right.

While the car is moving, they hear a siren from an ambulance. Henry looks at the rear mirror and finds an ambulance is coming up behind him.

P: What do we need to do now? Do we need to drive faster?

H: No. We have to slow down and pull over to make way for the ambulance.

P: Got it. I won't be nervous if I encounter the same situation again next time.

D: If all drivers yield the righ-of-way to the ambulance, that will reduce the incidence of accidents.

H: You bet.

I. Vocabulary words and phrases

1.	fasten	[ˋfæsn]	繫緊
2.	intersection	[ˌɪntɚˋsɛkʃən]	十字路口
3.	siren	[ˋsaɪrən]	警報器
4.	encounter	[ɪnˋkaʊntɚ]	遇到
5.	yield	[jild]	服從
6.	incidence	[ˋɪnsədns]	發生率

7.	next to	在 ... 旁邊
8.	seat belt	安全帶
9.	intend to	打算
10.	rear mirror	後視鏡
11.	come up	走近
12.	pull over	把 ... 開到路邊
13.	You bet.	當然

II. Answering the following questions

1. Where are they going?

2. When seeing the sign, Right Lane must Turn Right, what do drivers on the right lane need to do?

3. When hearing a siren from an ambulance coming up from behind, what does a driver need to do?

Pedestrians Have the Right of Way

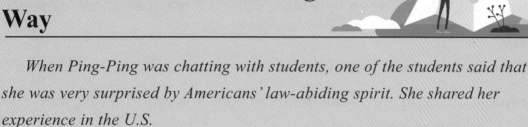

When Ping-Ping was chatting with students, one of the students said that she was very surprised by Americans' law-abiding spirit. She shared her experience in the U.S.

P: How is your internship going? Do you enjoy your life in the U.S.?

Emma: Yes, I do. I like to work with American students. In this, I can have a chance to practice English.

P: Do you think your English is better than before?

Emma: Yes, it is. And I hope I can keep making good progress.

P: I believe you can. Are there any interesting events happening so far?

Emma: Of course. But the most impressive thing I've ever seen is crossing the street.

P: Why?

Emma: I used to stop at the crosswalk. After the vehicles drove through, I would cross the street. But, here in the U.S., whenever I want to cross the street, the driver will stop their car and let me go first. Why?

P: I forgot to tell you that pedestrians have the right of way in the U.S. Most drivers abide by the rules strictly. Violators will be fined heavily.

Emma: At the beginning, I felt embarrassed crossing the street before the car. Now, I'm getting used to it. And, many drivers would smile at me when they were waiting. I feel they show respect with their manners.

P: I understand your feeling.

Emma: If drivers gave pedestrians the right of way in Taiwan, that would be great.

P: Actually, there's a law saying that pedestrians do have the right of way in Taiwan.

Emma: Then, why do drivers always take the right of way over pedestrians?

D: In my opinion, it's okay for drivers to take the right of way in the heavy traffic. But, they do need to respect pedestrians and give them the right of way when the traffic is light.

Emma: Although pedestrians have the right of way, they should walk faster. Otherwise there will be traffic jams on busy streets.

P: You're quite right!

I. Vocabulary words and phrases

1.	pedestrian	[pə`dɛstrɪən]	行人
2.	spirit	[`spɪrɪt]	精神
3.	impressive	[ɪm`prɛsɪv]	予人深刻印象的
4.	crosswalk	[`krɔsˌwɔk]	行人穿越道
5.	vehicle	[`viɪk!]	車輛
6.	strictly	[`strɪktlɪ]	嚴厲地

7.	violator	[`vaɪəˌletɚ]	違背者
8.	otherwise	[`ʌðɚˌwaɪz]	否則
9.	the right of way	優先權	
10.	used to	過去經常	
11.	abide by	遵守	
12.	get used to	漸漸習慣於	
13.	in my opinion	按照我的看法	
14.	traffic jam	交通阻塞	

II. Answering the following questions

1. Why does Emma like to work with American students?

2. What happened to Emma when she was crossing a street?

3. What does 'pedestrians have the right of way' mean?

Toy Train Depot

Ding-Ding and Ping-Ping took a morning walk in the neighboring park. They found a toy train. They were curious and walked to it.

D: Look. There's a train over there. Let's go take a look.

P: It's a toy train depot. How fun!

D: It's like a real train station equipped with a train car, railroad tracks, a platform, a railroad crossing and many warning signs.

P: It's very helpful to teach small kids the safety of taking the train with models.

D: Yes, it is. Let's see what they are.

P: Now, we are approaching the railroad crossing. The sign says, 'Stop, Look, and Listen'. It's exactly the same as how we were taught to cross the railroad in Taiwan.

D: Yes. The rule is a universal standard.

P: The sign warns passengers not to board until departure is called. Don't we get on the train once it completely stops?

D: Yeah, we do. Maybe in the old days, the train would roll and cause injury. Either way, we still need to be cautious.

P: When reading the signs, it seems that childhood memories come back.

D: I don't remember if there were many warning signs posted in the train station or not. However, I do remember clearly that schoolteachers always reminded us to keep our arms inside the train and to keep some distance from railroad tracks.

P: Yes, and when approaching the railroad crossing, we have to slow the car down and look both ways before starting to drive.

D: Yes, it is really important to obey the rules.

P: Having a park equipped with a toy train depot is good for parents to teach their children by playing.

D: Yes. I hope there are some of these models in Taiwan as well.

I. Vocabulary words and phrases

1.	depot	[`dipo]	火車站
2.	equip	[ɪ`kwɪp]	配備
3.	platform	[`plæt͵fɔrm]	月臺
4.	model	[`mɑd!]	模型
5.	approach	[ə`protʃ]	靠近
6.	universal	[͵junə`vɝs!]	普遍的
7.	board	[bord]	上（船，車，飛機等）
8.	departure	[dɪ`partʃɚ]	離開
9.	cautious	[`kɔʃəs]	十分小心的
10.	railroad track		鐵軌
11.	railroad crossing		鐵路平交道
12.	slow down		減低速度

II. Answering the following questions

1. Where is the toy train depot?

2. What is the toy train depot equipped with?

3. When people are approaching the railroad crossing, what do they need to do?

In the Park

Ding-Ding and Ping-Ping are used to taking a walk in the park every morning in Taiwan. Luckily, there is a park near their neighborhood in the U.S. Thus, they can do their regular exercise as usual.

D: It's seven o'clock now and there are only a few people in the park at this hour.

P: Maybe they are still in bed. Or maybe they prefer doing exercise at home.

D: It's very interesting that people from different cultures have different living habits.

P: Yeah, in Taiwan, many elderly people like to get up early and do some light exercise in the park. By doing exercise, they also have social activity with their neighbors or friends. But here, I see nobody! I mean, no seniors.

D: Yes, it's very quiet here. I'm curious as to what elderly people do in the morning. Don't they like to exercise?

P: That's a very good question. We'll look into it later.

D: Do you see that sign? It says that the park opens at dawn and closes at dusk. Maybe it's still early so there are not many people yet.

P: That sign says that people are not allowed to trespass during closing hours or else they will be prosecuted.

D: The regulation is very strict. My American friend once told me that alcoholic beverages are not allowed in the park. When he told me that, I thought he was exaggerating. Now, I see it's true.

P: There's no restriction like that in Taiwan, right?

D: No. But I think it's for security.

P: The park is so spacious. Do you think that vehicles can drive in?

D: No. Don't you see the sign? It's forbidden unless they have a permit.

P: Look, there's a guy walking his dog over there.

D: That dog is very cute and obedient.

P: Yeah, the dog owner has the dog on a leash. And he is cleaning up after his pet.

D: What a law-abiding citizen he is!

P: I wish our dog, Kiwi, were here too. I miss him.

D: Well, it's time to go home. You can Skype Kiwi if you want.

Ⅰ. Vocabulary words and phrases

1.	dawn	[dɔn]	黎明
2.	dusk	[dʌsk]	黃昏
3.	prosecute	[`prɑsɪˏkjut]	告發
4.	strict	[strɪkt]	嚴格的
5.	alcoholic	[ˏælkə`hɔlɪk]	含酒精的
6.	exaggerate	[ɪg`zædʒəˏret]	誇大
7.	restriction	[rɪ`strɪkʃən]	約束
8.	forbid	[fɚ`bɪd]	禁止

9.	obedient	[əˋbidjənt]	服從的
10.	citizen	[ˋsɪtəzn]	市民
11.	be used to		習慣於
12.	as usual		像往常一樣
13.	look into		調查
14.	on a leash		用皮帶拴著

II. Answering the following questions

1. Why do elderly people like to go to the park in the morning in Taiwan?

2. When are people not allowed to trespass in the park?

3. What do pet owners need to do when they walk their dog in the park?

Practice

IV-1

1.	dump	[dʌmp]	傾倒；垃圾場
2.	motor	[`motɚ]	馬達，發動機
3.	vehicle	[`viɪk!]	運載工具；車輛
4.	allow	[əˋlaʊ]	允許，准許

📌 What are people not allowed to do?

📌 Can the cyclist ride on this road?

IV-2

1.	load	[lod]	裝，裝載
2.	unload	[ʌn`lod]	卸貨，卸客
3.	flasher	[`flæʃɚ]	閃光物；閃爍器

📌 What do drivers do in this area?

📌 When do the drivers need to use the flasher in this area?

IV-3

1.	thru	[θru]	=through
2.	traffic	[`træfɪk]	交通；車輛

📌 What does the sign mean?

IV-4

| 1. | exit | [`ɛksɪt] | 出口，通道 |
| 2. | enter | [`ɛntɚ] | 進入；參加 |

📌 What does the sign mean?

📌 What does 'exit' mean?

IV-5

| 1. | beyond | [bɪˋjɑnd] | 在…的那一邊；越過 |
| 2. | point | [pɔɪnt] | （空間的）一點，處，地方，位置 |

What does the sign mean?

IV-6

| 1. | lane | [len] | 巷，弄；車道 |

📌 What does the sign mean?

IV-7

1.	peripheral	[pəˋrɪfərəl]	圓周的；周圍的；外面的
2.	control	[kənˋtrol]	控制；支配；管理
3.	zone	[zon]	地帶；地區

What does the sign mean?

IV-8

| 1. | central | [`sɛntrəl] | 中心的，中央的 |

📌 What does the sign mean?

IV-9

1.	castle	[ˋkæs!]	城堡；城堡式建築，巨宅
2.	except	[ɪkˋsɛpt]	除…之外
3.	authorized	[ˋɔθəˏraɪzd]	經授權的；經批准的；公認的
4.	as usual		像往常一樣

📌 What is the name of this building?

📌 What time is the car park closed?

📌 Who are allowed to park?

IV-10

| 1. | traffic | [`træfɪk] | 交通;車輛 |

What does the sign 'All Traffic MUST Turn Right' mean?

IV-11

📌 What does the sign mean?

IV-12

| 1. | turn | [tɝn] | 使轉動，使旋轉 |

What can't drivers do when the traffic light is red?

IV-13

1.	south	[saʊθ]	南；南方
2.	detour	[`ditʊr]	繞道；繞行的路

Where is it?

What do the drivers need to do in this street?

IV-14

📌 What does the sign mean?

IV-15

1.	outlet	[ˋaʊtˌlɛt]	出口

What does it mean when you see this sign?

IV-16

What does the sign mean?

IV-17

1.	M.P.H.	=mile per hour

★ What is the sign for?

★ When the drivers see the sign, what do they need to do?

IV-18

1.	button	[ˋbʌtn]	按鈕；鈕扣
2.	signal	[ˋsɪgn!]	信號；暗號

📌 Why do people push the button?

📌 When the walk signal is on, what does it mean?

IV-19

1.	weight	[wet]	重，重量；體重
2.	limit	[`lɪmɪt]	界限；限度；限制
3.	ton	[tʌn]	噸；公噸

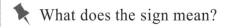 What does the sign mean?

IV-20

1.	closed	[klozd]	關閉的；封閉的
2.	ahead	[ə`hɛd]	在前；向前；預先，事前

📌 What does the sign mean?

📌 When the driver sees this sign, what does he/she need to do?

IV-21

When the driver sees 'no right turn ahead', what does he/she need to do?

IV-22

1.	pedestrian	[pə`dɛstrɪən]	步行者，行人
2.	three-way	[ˌθri`we]	三方面的；有三人參加的
3.	intersection	[ˌɪntɚ`sɛkʃən]	交叉點；道路交叉口；十字路口
4.	hill	[hɪl]	小山；丘陵；（道路等的）斜坡
5.	three-way stop intersection		三向停車交叉口

📌 What does the road look like when you see this sign?

📌 Who needs to be cautious?

📌 Why?

IV-23

1.	bus stop	公車的停車站

📌 What does the sign on the top mean?

📌 What does the sign in the middle mean?

📌 What does the sign at the bottom mean?

IV-24

| 1. | walkway | [ˋwɔkˌwe] | 走道；通道 |
| 2. | campus | [ˋkæmpəs] | 校園，校區 |

Where is the walkway bound?

IV-25

What does the sign mean?

IV-26

1.	pedestrian	[pə`dɛstrɪən]	步行者，行人
2.	staff	[stæf]	（全體）職員，（全體）工作人員

📌 What does the driver need to do, when he/she sees the sign above?

📌 Who can park, based on the sign below?

IV-1

1.	present	[ˈprɛznt]	在場的
2.	citation	[saɪˋteʃən]	引用；引證；列舉
3.	subject to		使服從於 ...；取決於

📌 What zone is it?

📌 In what situation, what activities are not allowed to do in this zone?

IV-28

1.	railroad	[`rel͵rod]	鐵路
2.	crossing	[`krɔsɪŋ]	交叉；交叉點，十字路口
3.	railroad crossing	鐵路平交道	

What does the sign mean?

What do the drivers need to do when they see the sign?

IV-29

1.	board	[bord]	上（船，車，飛機等）
2.	departure	[dɪ`partʃɚ]	離開；出發，起程
3.	roll	[rol]	滾動；打滾
4.	cause	[kɔz]	導致，使發生，引起
5.	injury	[`ɪndʒərɪ]	傷害；損害

When can people board?

Why does a train cause injury?

IV-30

| 1. | track | [træk] | 行蹤;軌道;足跡 |

 When the drivers are at the railroad crossing, what do they need to do?

 How many tracks does the sign indicate?

IV-31

NOTICE
For Your Safety
Keep 20 Ft. From
Railroad Tracks

1.	notice	[`notɪs]	公告，通知，貼示
2.	safety	[`seftɪ]	安全，平安
3.	railroad	[`rel͵rod]	鐵路；鐵路公司
4.	track	[træk]	行蹤；軌道；足跡
5.	Ft.	=foot(feet) 英尺	
6.	railroad track	鐵軌	

Why do people need to keep themselves from the railroad tracks?

What do people need to stay away from, and how far?

1.	serious	[`sɪrɪəs]	嚴重的;危急的;嚴肅的,莊嚴的
2.	injury	[`ɪndʒərɪ]	(對人,動物的)傷害;(對健康的)損害;(精神上的)傷害;損人的事
3.	result	[rɪ`zʌlt]	發生,產生;結果;導致
4.	responsible	[rɪ`spɑnsəb!]	需負責任的,承擔責任的
5.	accident	[`æksədənt]	事故;災禍

What may happen if persons are on or near track?

If accidents or injuries happen, who will be responsible?

IV-33

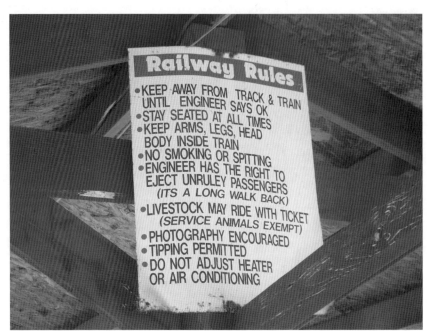

1.	engineer	[ˌɛndʒəˋnɪr]	工程師，技師；機械工；輪機手
2.	spit	[spɪt]	吐口水；吐痰
3.	eject	[ɪˋdʒɛkt]	逐出，轟出，驅逐
4.	unruly	[ʌnˋrulɪ]	難駕馭的，任性的，不守規矩的
5.	passenger	[ˋpæsndʒɚ]	乘客，旅客
6.	livestock	[ˋlaɪvˌstɑk]	家畜
7.	exempt	[ɪgˋzɛmpt]	免除，豁免
8.	photography	[fəˋtɑgrəfɪ]	照相術，攝影術
9.	encouraged	[ɪnˋkɝɪdʒd]	受到鼓舞的
10.	tip	[tɪp]	給小費
11.	adjust	[əˋdʒʌst]	校正；校準；調整
12.	heater	[ˋhitɚ]	加熱器，暖氣機

13.	keep away from	不靠近某人或某事物
14.	stay seated	保持坐姿
15.	at all times	隨時，永遠
16.	air conditioning	空氣調節

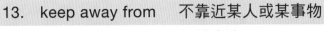 What are passengers not allowed to do in the train?

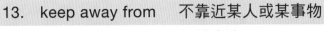 Where do passengers stay when they are taking the train?

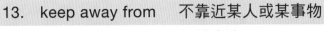 What kinds of passengers will be ejected from the train?

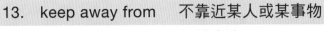 What animals can ride without ticket?

IV-34

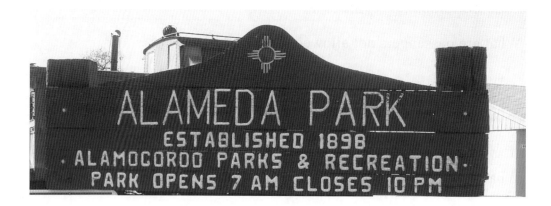

| 1. | establish | [ə`stæblɪʃ] | 建立；設立；創辦；確立 |
| 2. | recreation | [ˌrɛkrɪ`eʃən] | 消遣；娛樂，遊戲 |

📌 What is the name of the park?

📌 When was it founded?

📌 When are its opening hours?

IV-35

NO TRESPASSING
PROPERTY OF THE
CITY OF ALAMOGORDO
VIOLATORS WILL BE PROSECUTED

1.	trespass	[`trɛspəs]	擅自進入
2.	property	[`prɑpə·tɪ]	財產，資產；所有物
3.	violator	[`vaɪə‚letə·]	違背者；褻瀆者；侵犯者
4.	prosecute	[`prɑsɪ‚kjut]	對…起訴；告發；依法進行

📌 What does the sign mean?

📌 Who owns the property?

📌 If people don't follow the sign, what will happen?

IV-36

> **Closes At Dusk**
> **No Trespassing**
> **City Of Alamogordo**

| 1. | dusk | [dʌsk] | 薄暮，黃昏；幽暗 |

📌 What does the sign mean?

📌 When will the place close?

📌 Where is the place located?

IV-37

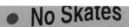

- No Skates
- No Skate Boards
- No Bicycles
- One Person On Swing-
  At A Time

1.	skate	[sket]	冰鞋；四輪溜冰鞋
2.	skateboard	[`sketˌbord]	滑板
3.	swing	[swɪŋ]	鞦韆；盪鞦韆
4.	at a time		依次，逐一，每次；曾經

What activities can't people do?

How many persons can be on the swing at a time?

IV-38

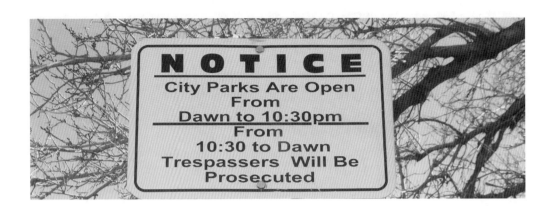

NOTICE
City Parks Are Open
From
Dawn to 10:30pm
From
10:30 to Dawn
Trespassers Will Be
Prosecuted

1.	dawn	[dɔn]	黎明，拂曉
2.	trespasser	[ˈtrɛspəsɚ]	侵害者；違反者；侵入者
3.	prosecute	[ˈprɑsɪˌkjut]	對…起訴；告發；依法進行

When are the city parks open?

When can't people stay in the parks?

IV-39

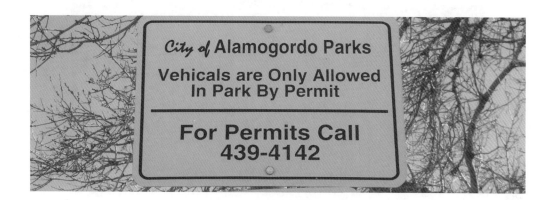

City of **Alamogordo Parks**

**Vehicals are Only Allowed
In Park By Permit**

**For Permits Call
439-4142**

1.	vehicle	[`viɪk!]	車輛；飛行器；傳播媒介；工具，手段
2.	permit	[`pɝ-mɪt]	許可證

How are vehicles allowed to park?

How do drivers get permits?

IV-40

Facility Use Is On A First Come First Serve Basis

Except By Permitted **Reservations**

For Permits Call The Alamogordo Family Recreation Center At 439-4142

1.	facility	[fə`sɪlətɪ]	設備，設施；工具
2.	basis	[`besɪs]	基礎，根據；準則
3.	permit	[pə`mɪt]	允許，許可，准許
4.	reservation	[ˌrɛzə`veʃn]	保留（意見）；（公共）專用地；禁獵區；自然保護區
5.	recreation	[ˌrɛkrɪ`eʃn]	消遣；娛樂，遊戲

What basis is facility use on?

Who can have exception?

How to get a permit?

IV-41

1.	attention	[əˋtɛnʃən]	注意；注意力；專心
2.	alcoholic	[ˏælkəˋhɔlɪk]	酒精的；含酒精的；由酒精引起的
3.	beverage	[ˋbɛvərɪdʒ]	飲料
4.	ordinance	[ˋɔrdɪnəns]	法令；條令；條例
5.	public place		公共場所

📌 What does the sign mean?

📌 What is the rule based on?

📌 What is the title of the rule?

實用英文

IV-42

1.	beware	[bɪˋwɛr]	注意，提防；當心，小心
2.	pickpocket	[ˋpɪkˏpɑkɪt]	扒手
3.	loose	[lus]	放蕩的，荒淫的；鬆的，寬的；鬆散的
4.	loose women	蕩婦	

🔖 What does this sign mean?

🔖 What kinds of people are mentioned in this sign?

IV-43

1.	owner	[ˋonɚ]	物主；所有人
2.	leash	[liʃ]	（用皮帶等）栓住，繫住；約束，控制
3.	waste	[west]	排泄物；廢（棄）物；廢料
4.	threat	[θrɛt]	威脅，恐嚇
5.	degraded	[dɪˋgredɪd]	被降級職的；墮落的；已失名譽的
6.	transmit	[trænsˋmɪt]	傳送，傳達；傳（光、熱、聲等）
7.	disease	[dɪˋziz]	病，疾病
8.	clean up		打掃；整理；清理，清除，整理

📌 Who asks pet owners to do something for their pets?

📌 What do pet owners need to do to their pets in the park?

📌 What problems does the pet waste cause?

IV-44

| 1. | penalty | [`pɛn!tɪ] | 處罰；刑罰；罰款 |

📌 What does the sign mean?

📌 What is the maximum penalty?

Campus Life

校園生活

College Life

Arlin is a doctoral student studying at a university in the U.S. She lives in a dormitory and shares the room with an American undergraduate student, Rita. Today, she has an appointment with her advisor, Dr. Hudson, at 10:00am. Afterwards, she is having lunch with Rita in the dining hall.

A: Good morning. You're up early today.

R: I have class at 9:00am. I'd better hurry up. I couldn't fall asleep until midnight because it was noisy last night.

A: Really? I didn't hear it. I fell asleep in a minute because I was so tired from studying. What happened?

R: Two girls were fighting and making loud noises outside our room. I cannot believe the noise didn't bother you at all.

A: I'm lucky – I'm a person who sleeps well all the time and under any circumstances. I have a meeting with my professor this morning. How about having lunch together?

R: OK, talk to you later.

Arlin goes to see Dr. Hudson. Her office is in a building next to the library. When Arlin arrives, Dr. Hudson is already expecting her.

A: Good morning, Dr. Hudson.

H: Good morning. How are you today?

A: Fine. You are taking pills. Are you sick?

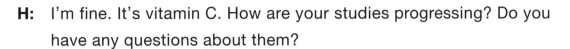

H: I'm fine. It's vitamin C. How are your studies progressing? Do you have any questions about them?

A: Yes, I've got some questions and I need your help.

One hour later, their meeting is over. Arlin is leaving the office.

A: Thank you, Dr. Hudson, for you time and kindness.

H: You're welcome. I'll see you in class.

Arlin leaves Dr. Hudson's office and goes to find the restroom. A sign shows its location. It's nearly time for lunch and Arlin walks to the dining hall.

A: Hi, Rita. How was your class? You still look tired.

R: Like I said, I didn't sleep well last night, so I couldn't concentrate in the class.

A: Poor girl. You need some nutritious food to give you energy. Let's go in and see what we can have for lunch.

I. Vocabulary words and phrases

1.	doctoral	[ˈdɑktərəl]	博士的
2.	dormitory	[ˈdɔrməˌtorɪ]	學生宿舍
3.	undergraduate	[ˌʌndəˈgrædʒʊɪt]	大學生
4.	appointment	[əˈpɔɪntmənt]	（會面的）約定
5.	advisor	[ədˈvaɪzə]	指導教授
6.	afterwards	[ˈæftəwədz]	後來
7.	progress	[prəˈgrɛs]	進展
8.	concentrate	[ˈkɑnsɛnˌtret]	全神貫注
9.	nutritious	[njuˈtrɪʃəs]	有營養的

10.	dining hall	食堂
11.	fall asleep	睡著
12.	under any circumstances	無論任何情況
13.	next to	在 ... 旁邊

II. Answering the following questions

1. Where does Arlin live while she is studying in the U.S.?

2. Why can't Rita sleep well?

3. What is Arlin going to do in the morning?

In the Library

Arlin has a routine of going to the library and studying there every day. She is working on her paper in her study carrel and a Taiwanese student comes to talk to her.

A: Hi. How are you doing? I haven't seen you for a while. Have you gotten used to the life here?

S: I'm still trying to adjust. I can't cook and I don't like the food they serve in the cafeteria. It makes my stomach upset.

A: It takes time. How's your schoolwork going?

S: It's problematic. I can't understand the professors' lectures. I need to improve my listening skills. I feel frustrated and just awful.

A: Take it easy. I had a similar situation when I started studying in the U.S. Time is the best medicine to cure this. But of course, you need to study hard too.

S: OK, I'll get back to work. Talk to you later.

Later on, Arlin goes to find a computer to search for information on the Internet. A guy, Craig, sitting next to her smiles at her and asks her a question.

C: Excuse me. I can't figure this out. Could you tell me what this is?

A: Let me see. Oh, 'R' means Thursday. It's shorthand for one of the days of the week. And 'T' means Tuesday.

C: Oh, yes. Why can't I understand it? Thank you very much. My name is Craig. What's your name? And where are you from?

A: I'm Arlin. I'm from Taiwan. I'm a doctoral student in the English program.

C: Nice to meet you. I major in music.

After their conversation, Arlin goes to a bookshelf to look for books she needs. Then, she walks to the circulation desk.

A: I'd like to check out these books.

Librarian: May I have your student ID?

A: Here it is.

Librarian: OK. They are due on October 15th. And you may renew them if you want. You can see the books you've checked out, their due dates and their renewal status from your library account.

A: Got it. Thank you very much.

I. Vocabulary words and phrases

1.	routine	[ruˋtin]	例行公事
2.	carrel	[ˋkærəl]	（圖書館）個人閱讀小單間
3.	adjust	[əˋdʒʌst]	調整
4.	cafeteria	[ˌkæfəˋtɪrɪə]	自助餐館
5.	problematic	[ˌprɑbləˋmætɪk]	問題的
6	lecture	[ˋlɛktʃɚ]	授課
7.	shorthand	[ˋʃɔrtˌhænd]	簡略的表達方式
8.	bookshelf	[ˋbʊkˌʃɛlf]	書架

9.	circulation	[ˌsɝkjəˋleʃən]	循環
10.	librarian	[laɪˋbrɛrɪən]	圖書館員
11.	due	[dju]	到期的
12.	renew	[rɪˋnju]	更新
13.	status	[ˋstetəs]	情形
14.	search for		尋找
15.	on the Internet		在網上
16.	major in		主修
17.	check out		結帳離開

II. Answering the following questions

1. What problems does the Taiwanese student have?

2. Why does Craig ask Arlin for help?

3. When checking out the library books, what do students need to show?

Lesson 16

Being a Germ Buster

When the coronavirus was breaking out, it caused panic around the world. TV news stations kept giving updates on the frightening events. However, it also taught people how to be germ busters. Ding-Ding and Ping-Ping were talking about the coronavirus.

D: The outbreak has lasted for months and it seems like it won't stop.

P: Can you believe that I get depressed whenever I hear the news?

D: I saw that there was a long line outside a pharmacy yesterday. Many people were waiting to buy masks for themselves and their families.

P: It's very interesting. Wearing a mask used to be a stereotype for Asians. I remember once I went to visit my American friend and stayed at her place for few days. Her husband had a cold and kept coughing seriously. She asked him to wear a mask and her husband rejected the idea.

D: Why? Isn't it good manners to wear a mask when people get sick?

P: That's our thinking. Maybe they think it's funny to do it.

D: Actually, we need to protect ourselves during this emergency and cooperate with people who are working on epidemic prevention.

P: When I go into a school or any institution, someone takes my temperature with a forehead thermometer.

D: You know what? I need to go to another city to do business once a week by bus. Passengers are required to wear masks, have their temperatures taken, and use alcohol hand sanitizer before getting on the bus.

P: It's a lot of trouble dealing with the disease. I hope it goes away as soon as possible.

D: Actually, we are lucky. We can still walk around the streets. In some countries, people are almost losing their patience being quarantined.

P: You are right. Some of my friends have suggested getting together after the crisis is over. I hope I can meet them as soon as possible.

D: Who doesn't? No matter what, we still need to keep a safe distance from each other.

P: OK. I'd better wash my hands thoroughly. I've touched lots of things while chatting with you.

I. Vocabulary words and phrases

1.	coronavirus	[kə`rounə͵vaɪrəs]	冠狀病毒
2.	panic	[`pænɪk]	恐慌
3.	update	[ʌp`det]	更新
4.	germ	[dʒɝm]	細菌
5.	buster	[`bʌstɚ]	破壞者
6.	outbreak	[`aut͵brek]	爆發
7.	last	[læst]	持續
8.	pharmacy	[`farməsɪ]	藥局
9.	mask	[mæsk]	口罩

10.	stereotype	[ˈstɛrɪəˌtaɪp]	刻板印象
11.	cough	[kɔf]	咳嗽
12.	reject	[rɪˈdʒɛkt]	拒絕
13.	temperature	[ˈtɛmprətʃɚ]	溫度
14.	forehead	[ˈfɔrˌhɛd]	前額
15.	thermometer	[θɚˈmɑmətɚ]	溫度計
16.	sanitizer	[ˈsænəˌtaɪzɚ]	衛生洗滌劑
17.	patience	[ˈpeʃəns]	耐心
18.	quarantine	[ˈkwɔrənˌtin]	隔離
19.	crisis	[ˈkraɪsɪs]	危機
20.	thoroughly	[ˈθɚˌolɪ]	徹底地
21.	break out		爆發
22.	get depressed		沮喪
23.	epidemic prevention		防疫
24.	as soon as possible		盡快

Ⅱ. Answering the following questions

1. Why does Ping-Ping feel depressed?

2. Why do people wear masks?

3. Before getting on a bus, what do passengers need to do?

Practice

V-1

TO USE ELEVATOR
PLEASE CALL ON PHONE LOCATED BY FRONT DOORS TO WALLACE DORMITORY. OPEN BLACK BOX, PUSH BLACK BUTTON FOR DIAL TONE, DIAL 7-2295 AND SOMEONE WILL ASSIST YOU.

1.	elevator	[`ɛləˏvetɚ]	電梯；升降機；起重機，起卸機
2.	locate	[lo`ket]	使…座落於；把…設置在
3.	dormitory	[`dɔrməˏtorɪ]	學生宿舍
4.	dial	[`daɪəl]	撥號，打電話
5.	assist	[ə`sɪst]	幫助，協助

What do people need to do if they need to use the elevator?

Where is the phone located?

How to use the phone?

V-2

1.	campus	[ˋkæmpəs]	校園，校區
2.	sidewalk	[ˋsaɪd͵wɔk]	人行道
3.	public	[ˋpʌblɪk]	公眾，民眾
4.	construction	[kənˋstrʌkʃən]	建造，建設；建築物，建造物
5.	due to		因為，由於

Who is the campus sidewalks closed to?

Why is the campus sidewalks closed?

V-3

ACCESS FOR THE DISABLED IS AVAILABLE AT THE REAR OF THE BUILDING

1.	disabled	[dɪs`eb!d]	殘廢的；有缺陷的
2.	available	[ə`veləb!]	可用的；可得到的
3.	rear	[rɪr]	後部，後面；背後，背面；撫養，培養

How do the disabled gain access to the building?

V-4

OFFICE HOURS:
8:00 AM-12:00 NOON
1:00 PM-4:30 PM

SUMMER HOURS:
8:00 AM-12:00 NOON
12:30 PM-4:00 PM

1.	office hours	上班時間

What time will the office be closed?

What are the similarity and difference between office hours and summer hours?

V-5

1.	recycle	[ri`saɪk!]	使再循環；再利用
2.	plastic	[`plæstɪk]	塑膠的；塑膠製的；可塑的，塑像的
3.	can	[kæn]	（食物）罐頭；金屬容器
4.	on the go		隨時隨地；活躍，忙碌

📌 What are three recycling items?

📌 Why do people recycle?

V-6

For your Health & Safety this Window is restricted to only open 100mm

Do not try and force the window to open further or disengage the restrictor

All broken or damaged windows will be charged for.

1.	restrict	[rɪˋstrɪkt]	限制；限定；約束
2.	mm=millimeter	[ˋmɪləˏmitɚ]	公釐，毫米
3.	force	[fors]	強行打開；強迫；用力推進
4.	further	[ˋfɝðɚ]	更遠地；進一步地；深一層地
5.	disengage	[ˏdɪsɪnˋgedʒ]	解開，解除；使脫離
6.	damage	[ˋdæmɪdʒ]	損害，毀壞
7.	charge	[tʃɑrdʒ]	索價；收費
8.	restrictor		限流器；閘板

✎ Why does the window only open 100mm?

✎ What does the sign mean?

✎ If people break or damage the window, what will happen to them?

V-7

1.	assembly	[əˈsɛmblɪ]	與會者;（為了特定目的）聚集在一起的人;集會;集合
2.	authorized	[ˈɔθəˌraɪzd]	經授權的;經批准的;公認的
3.	access	[ˈæksɛs]	接近,進入;進入的權利;使用
4.	in progress		進行中

📌 Why do people need to be quiet?

📌 Who can access to the show?

V-8

ADDITIONAL
RESTROOMS
LOCATED ON
FIRST FLOOR

1.	additional	[ə`dɪʃən!]	額外的；附加的；添加的
2.	locate	[lo`ket]	使…座落於；把…設置在

Where are additional restrooms?

V-9

RESTROOMS LOCATED
← — near staircases — →
and on the first floor

| 1. | staircase | [`stɛrˌkes] | 樓梯；樓梯間 |

📌 Where are the restrooms located?

📌 Where are the staircases?

V-10

> Last to leave?
> Help us conserve energy
> Please turn off the lights
> UW Facilities Services Department
> NE Maintenance Zone 685-8815

1.	conserve	[kən`sɝv]	保存；保護；節省；將…做成蜜餞
2.	energy	[`ɛnədʒɪ]	能量；活力，幹勁；精力，能力
3.	maintenance	[`mentənəns]	維持，保持；維修，保養
4.	turn off		關掉

📌 Who does the sign remind of?

📌 How to conserve energy?

📌 Who made this sign?

V-11

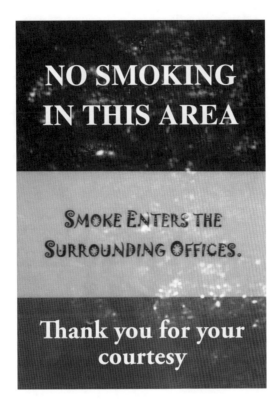

NO SMOKING IN THIS AREA

SMOKE ENTERS THE SURROUNDING OFFICES.

Thank you for your courtesy

1.	surrounding	[sə`raʊndɪŋ]	周圍的；附近的
2.	courtesy	[`kɝtəsɪ]	禮貌；謙恭有禮的言辭（或舉動）

 What does the sign mean?

V-12

In case of fire
do not use elevators

Use stairways

Elevators out of
service
during emergencies

1.	elevator	[ˈɛləˌvetɚ]	電梯；升降機；起重機，起卸機
2.	stairway	[ˈstɛrˌwe]	樓梯，階梯
3.	emergency	[ɪˈmɝdʒənsɪ]	緊急情況；突然事件；非常時刻
4.	in case of		假如碰上；如果發生；假使；萬一
5.	out of service		不被使用，停用
6.	get out of service	退役，退伍	

What can't people use when a building is on fire?

What can people use when they cannot use elevators?

What will be out of service during emergencies?

PLEASE
LOCK **THE DOOR**
AND
ARM **THE ALARM**

-after 7pm Weekdays
-at all times on Weekends

1.	lock	[lɑk]	鎖，鎖上
2.	arm	[ɑrm]	武裝；備戰
3.	alarm	[əˋlɑrm]	警報；警報器；鬧鐘（＝ alarm clock）
4.	at all times		每時每刻；永遠，一直

📌 When do people lock the door and arm the alarm on weekdays and weekends?

V-14

NO SMOKING EXCEPT IN DESIGNATED AREAS

| 1. | designated | [ˋdɛzɪgˌnetɪd] | 指定的，選定的 |

Where can people smoke?

V-15

PLEASE NOTE:

No journals are permitted in the study carrels or on any upper floor of the library.

1.	note	[not]	注意，注目；注意到
2.	journal	[ˋdʒɝn!]	日報；雜誌；期刊；日記；日誌
3.	carrel	[ˋkærəl]	（圖書館）個人閱讀小單間
4.	upper	[ˋʌpɚ]	較高的；上面的；上游的；內地的

Where are journals not permitted in?

Where is the study carrel?

V-16

| 1. | zone | [zon] | 地帶；地區；氣候帶；動植物分布帶 |
| 2. | respectful | [rɪˋspɛktfəl] | 恭敬的；尊敬人的，尊重人的 |

Why do people need to be respectful of others in the zone?

V-17

Please Limit Cell Phone Use to First and Ground Floor of Stapleton Library

1.	ground	[graʊnd]	土壤；土地；地面
2.	cell phone=cellular phone or mobile phone		行動電話，手機
3.	ground floor		（建築物的）底層；【英】公車的下層

📌 Where do people need to limit their cell phone use?

📌 Where is the ground floor in a building?

V-18

1.	restroom	[ˈrestruːm]	洗手間；休息室
2.	floor	[flor]	（樓房的）層；地板，地面

What time is the restroom cleaned?

If people need to use the restroom during cleaning time, what do they need to do?

V-19

1.	emergency	[ɪˋmɝdʒənsɪ]	緊急情況；突然事件；非常時刻
2.	exit	[ˋɛksɪt]	出口，通道；太平門
3.	alarm	[əˋlɑrm]	警報；警報器；鬧鐘
4.	sound	[saʊnd]	發聲，響起；發音；聽起來

📌 In what situation, people are allowed to take the exit?

📌 What happens if people use the exit?

V-20

Only Covered Drinks and Java City Food Permitted

| 1. | covered | [`kʌvəd] | 戴帽子的；有蓋的；隱蔽著的；有屋頂的 |

📌 What drinks are permitted to have?

📌 What food is permitted to have?

V-21

Please do not remove journals from this floor.

1.	remove…from	[rɪ`muv]	移動，搬開；調動；遷移，搬家

🔖 What things are not allowed to be removed from this floor?

🔖 What can't people do with the journals on this floor?

V-22

1.	germ	[dʒɝm]	微生物；細菌；病菌
2.	buster	[`bʌstɚ]	破壞者；有巨大破壞力的東西
3.	second	[`sɛkənd]	秒；第二的；二等的，次等的
4.	rinse	[rɪns]	沖洗；輕洗；潤絲
5.	towel	[`taʊəl]	毛巾，手巾；紙巾
6.	paper towel		紙巾

What does germ-buster mean?

How to stay away from germ?

After washing hands, how do people turn off water?

What are the steps of washing hands?

V-23

FREE FLU SHOTS
FOR FACULTY, STAFF, & STUDENTS!

When: Tuesday, January 21, 2014
Time: 4PM-6PM
When: Wednesday, January 22, 2014
Time: 2PM-5PM

Where: Student Union, MB 2110 (Old Game Room)

BRING CURRENT UTPB ID!

1.	flu	[flu]	流行性感冒
2.	shot	[ʃɑt]	注射；射擊，槍（砲）聲；【體】投籃；一擊
3.	faculty	[`fæk!tɪ]	（大學或院，系的）全體教職員
4.	staff	[stæf]	（全體）職員，（全體）工作人員
5.	union	[`junjən]	結合；合併；工會；聯合會，協會
6.	current	[`kɝənt]	現時的，當前的；現行的；通用的，流行的
7.	flu shot		流感注射
8.	student union		大學之學生活動大樓；（大專院校的）學生會
9.	ID=identification		身分證明；身分證

📌 Who is this sign for?

📌 What might people do when they see the sign?

📌 How much do people pay for the shots?

📌 Where do people go to take the shot?

📌 What do people need to bring with them for the shots?

IV-24

1.	cough	[kɔf]	咳嗽
2.	tissue	[`tɪʃʊ]	紙巾；面紙；衛生紙
3.	sneeze	[sniz]	打噴嚏
4.	sleeve	[sliv]	袖子；袖套
5.	alcohol	[`ælkəˌhɔl]	酒精；含酒精飲料；酒
6.	cleaner	[`klinɚ]	吸塵器；清潔劑；清潔工；乾洗工
7.	alcohol-based		以酒精為主成分的
8.	stay healthy		身體處於健康狀態

📌 Based on the sign, how do people stay healthy?

📌 When people want to cough or sneeze, what do they need to do?

📌 How do people clean their hands?

單元練習解答 ✒ Practice Answer

Part 1 | High-Speed Rail Station 高鐵站

I-1

📌 Where are people going to when they are taking the up-running escalator?

A: They are going to the upper floor.

I-2

📌 Who had better use the platform elevator?

A: People who are disabled, elderly, or pregnant. And, people who use the baby stroller or carry a large luggage.

I-3

📌 When is the departure time bound to 左營？

A: 9:46

📌 What platform is it?

A: It's 1B, southbound platform.

I-4

📌 How many cars are non-reserved?

A: 3

I-5

📌 Why could the floor be wet and slippery?

A: Due to the rain.

📌 What do people need to do when walking on the wet and slippery floor?

A: Watch their step.

I-6

📌 What does the sign mean?

A: In case of emergency, press the button to stop.

I-7

📌 What do people need to do if their ticket or any other items were fallen onto the HSR track area?

A: They can contact the station staff for assistance to retrieve the object.

📌 In what situation can people enter the HSR track area?

A: Under no circumstance.

📌 What will happen to people who enter the HSR track area?

A: It will result in a fine or criminal liability.

I-8

📌 What do people need to do if they fall onto the track?

A: They need to take refuge in the recess area and shout for help.

I-9

📌 What is OCS?

A: Overhead Catenary System.

📌 What do people need to ensure before using fire hydrant?

A: OCS is powered off.

I-10

📍 What does the sign mean?

A: Don't use unless in emergency.

I-11

📍 Where is the intercom?

A: In the housing.

📍 When do people use the intercom?

A: In case of emergency.

📍 After using the intercom, what do people need to do?

A: They need to replace the handset and close the housing door.

I-12

📍 When people need assistance, what can they do?

A: They can lift the handset to contact the station staff for assistance.

I-13

📍 What does the sign mean?

A: It shows where the fire hydrant is.

I-14

📍 What is the fire extinguisher for?

A: To put out a fire.

I-15

📍 What does the sign mean?

A: No smoking.

I-16

🔖 What is not allowed in the premises?

    A: Smoking.

🔖 What is the sign for?

    A: It tries to ask people not to smoke in the area and to abide by the smoke-free law.

I-17

🔖 Where do people escape from in case of an emergency?

    A: Through windows.

🔖 How do people escape from the window?

    A: They can break the window with a hammer.

🔖 Why do people escape from the window?

    A: For evacuation.

🔖 What does vandalism mean?

    A: It's an action of deliberately damaging public or private property.

I-18

🔖 What is the maximum load for the table?

    A: 10 kilograms.

I-19

🔖 Why do people switch their mobile phone to vibration mode?

    A: They try not to annoy other people.

🔖 What do people do when talking on the telephone?

    A: In a low voice.

I-20

🔖 What is not allowed in the train?

A: Smoking.

🔖 What will happen if people smoke in the train?

A: They are liable to a maximum fine of NT$10,000.

I-21

🔖 Why do people need to keep away from the vestibule door during operation?

A: For safety.

I-22

🔖 While standing, what do people need to do?

A: They need to hold the handgrip firmly.

I-23

🔖 When can people use the alarm?

A: In the case of a safety related emergency.

🔖 What will happen if the alarm is set for fun?

A: Violators will be fined up to NT$6000.

I-24

🔖 Where are you now?

A: In the car number 11.

I-25

🔖 When do people press the red button?

A: In emergency.

I-26

What does the sign tell people to do?

A: Buckle the belt after using it.

I-27

Where do people put their carry-on baggage?

A: Put it on the baggage rack.

Where do people keep their valuables?

A: They need to keep their valuables with them.

I-28

Who can take the priority seat?

A: The pregnant women, elderly, disabled and passengers with infant children.

I-29

What does it mean?

A: It is a passage between seats.

I-30

What is the maximum load?

A: 15 kilograms.

How does a mother secure her baby?

A: With the safety belt.

I-31

What does the sign mean?

A: Parents can change their babies' diapers on the table.

I-32

📌 What things can be disposed in the toilet?

    A: The toilet paper and seat-cover paper.

I-33

📌 Why do people need to place their hand over the sensor?

    A: To flush the toilet.

       How to flush the toilet?

    A: Place the hand over the sensor.

I-34

📌 What does the sign mean?

    A: The sensor can flush the toilet automatically.

I-35

📌 What is the hand dryer for?

    A: It can dry people's hands.

I-36

📌 What does the sign mean?

    A: To remind people of locking the door.

I-37

📌 Where is the spare toilet paper roll?

    A: It's inside.

📌 How to replace with a new toilet paper roll?

    A: Pull the lever.

📌 How to take care of the empty roll?

    A: Deposit it in the trash bin.

Part 2 │ Airportl Station 機場

II-1

📌 While people are standing in line, what do they need to be?

A: Be patient.

II-2

📌 When the green light is flashing, what do people need to do?

A: They need to proceed to the counter.

II-3

📌 What are LAGs?

A: Liquid, aerosol, and gel.

📌 What is the bin for?

A: To dispose LAGs.

II-4

📌 What is the security regulation on?

A: Hand luggage.

📌 Who needs to follow the regulation?

A: International bound passengers.

📌 Where are the liquid containers placed?

A: Clear plastic bags.

📌 How much can each liquid container hold?

A: 100ml/100gm/3.4oz.

📌 What is the maximum capacity in one bag?

A: 1 liter.

II-5

🔖 Why do people need to take off their belt or metal objects?

A: They may cause the alarm to sound.

🔖 What metal objects are mentioned?

A: Belt, keys, coins, and wrist watch.

II-6

🔖 Who needs to read the notice?

A: Passengers.

🔖 What things have the potential of being used to conceal explosives devices?

A: Electric and electronic devices.

🔖 What do people need to do if their hand luggage have electric or electronic devices?

A: They need to declare and separate them at the security check point.

II-7

🔖 What can't people flush away?

A: The sanitary products.

🔖 Why can't people practice on the flush handle?

A: It may be broken into pieces.

🔖 How do people do with the toilet?

A: Keep it dry.

🔖 What will happen if people smoke in the toilet?

A: People outside will break down the door to save them.

II-8

🔖 What thing can be disposed of in the bin?

A: Sanitary pads only.

🔖 How do people open the bin?

A: Step on the pedal of the bin.

II-9

🔖 What kind of hand dryer is it?

A: It is automatic.

🔖 Where do people put their hands if they want to dry their hands?

A: Under the blower.

II-10

🔖 What is the sanitizer for?

A: To clean the toilet seat.

🔖 How do people use the sanitizer?

A: Press the button.

II-11

🔖 What are the recycling items?

A: Paper, plastic, aluminum, and glass.

II-12

🔖 When seeing the sign, what can't people do?

A: Bring their pets with them.

🔖 What are the three kinds of pets showed in the sign?

A: Dog, cat, and mouse.

II-13

📌 What actions are not allowed on the conveyor belt?

A: Climb, walk, and ride.

📌 Who is monitoring this area?

A: It is under CCTV monitoring.

II-14

📌 Who does the warning give to?

A: People who are taking the escalator.

📌 What do people need to do while taking the escalator?

A: Hold handrail.

📌 Who needs to be supervised?

A: Children.

📌 Where should people stand?

A: Between yellow lines.

📌 Who are suggested taking a lift?

A: The disabled, elderly, and people with a luggage trolley.

II-15

📌 Why do people need to be cautious when seeing this sign?

A: To avoid the risk of electric shock.

II-16

📌 Who can take the priority seats based on the sign?

A: People who are disabled, elderly, pregnant women, and with a baby stroller.

II-17

🔖 Where aren't children allowed to sit if they have no adult's supervision?

    A: Near the rail.

🔖 Who will take the responsibility if any incidents happen?

    A: People who cause the incident by themselves.

II-18

🔖 In case of fire, who do people call?

    A: Airport Fire and Rescue Center or Airport Operation Center.

II-19

🔖 When do people need to use the fire alarm?

    A: When there is fire.

🔖 Why do people need to press hard?

    A: To break glass.

II-20

🔖 What does the sign mean?

    A: There're free e-books in the zone.

II-21

🔖 What do beverages contain?

    A: Wine, aperitif, spirit, liqueur, beer, and soft drink

🔖 What kind of beverage is Beefeater Gin?

    A: Spirit

📌 Based on the menu, what kind of beverage would you like to request?

A: The answer may vary.

II-22

📌 What is the difference between cocktail and mocktail?

A: The former one is alcoholic and the latter one non-alcoholic.

📌 What kinds of tea are there in the menu?

A: Black tea, jasmine tea, oolong tea, pu-erh tea, Sencha green tea, and peppermint tea.

📌 What kind of fruit juice do passengers have?

A: Orange, apple, pineapple, and tomato.

II-23

📌 What food do passengers have for breakfast?

A: Fruit, main course, bakery, and hot beverage.

📌 What do fried egg noodles include with?

A: Shredded char siew, prawns, and mushrooms.

📌 What kind of beverages will be served?

A: Coffee and (Chinese) tea.

II-24

📌 What food do passengers have for lunch?

A: Appetizer, main course, dessert, bakery, and hot beverage.

📌 What food would be served with the main course?

A: Sautéed vegetables and rosemary potatoes.

📌 What dessert will be served?

  A: Ice cream

II-25

📌 What is the difference between this menu and the previous one?

  A: The food served in this menu is oriental selection and the previous one is international selection.

📌 What food will be served with deep-fried pork?

  A: Honey pepper sauce, Chinese vegetable, and steamed rice.

📌 What will go with tea smoked duck?

  A: Marinated bean curd salad.

II-26

📌 What do they have for the main course?

  A: Mutton and chicken.

📌 What kind of desserts can passengers have?

  A: Coconut rice pudding and cheese and biscuits.

📌 What food will be served with mutton?

  A: Creamy mashed potato, seasoned broccoli, and red peppers.

II-27

📌 If passengers are hungry but meals are not being served, what can they do?

  A: They can ask for instant cup noodles.

II-28

📌 What is the menu about?

A: Savoury snack.

📌 What kind of snacks can passengers have?

A: Honey mustard chicken, chocolate muffin, and tea (or coffee).

📌 What will be filled with honey mustard flavored chicken and coleslaw salad?

A: Wholemeal panini bread roll.

II-29

📌 What are the main courses?

A: Sauteed beef and penne

📌 What kind of dessert will be served?

A: Honey cake

📌 What will be served before landing?

A: Yoghurt and assorted cheese.

II-30

📌 What food will go with scrambled eggs?

A: Sautéed mushrooms or roasted tomatoes.

📌 What will go with bread?

A: Butter or jam.

II-31

📌 To start with, what can passengers have?

A: Oriental coleslaw salad.

🔖 **What main dish can passengers choose?**

   A: Braised beef or grilled chicken.

🔖 **What snack will go after the main dish?**

   A: Baked honey cheese cake or soft roll.

II-32

🔖 **What can passengers have for breakfast at the beginning?**

   A: Seasonal fresh fruits.

🔖 **What food is served for breakfast?**

   A: Omelette, congee, and croissant.

🔖 **What is the meal prepared according to?**

   A: Islamic principles.

II-33

🔖 **How much do passengers pay for the beverages served throughout the flight?**

   A: They are free of charge.

🔖 **What kind of spirits are there?**

   A: Scotch whisky, gin, vodka, and brandy.

🔖 **What kind of beverages are there in the menu?**

   A: They are alcoholic drinks.

II-34

🔖 **How many non-alcoholic beverages are listed in the menu?**

   A: 13

🔖 **In addition to non-alcoholic beverages, what else are there?**

   A: Tea and coffee.

📌 Who can passengers ask for help?

A: The flight attendant.

II-35

📌 What can passengers have for the starter?

A: Fresh fruit.

📌 What are the main courses?

A: Braised chicken and pan-seared assorted seafood.

📌 What is steamed rice served with?

A: Braised chicken.

📌 What is fusilli pasta served with?

A: Pan-seared assorted seafood.

Part 3 | Accommodation & Meals 訂房及餐飲

III-1

📌 Where do people ring the bell?

A: At the front door.

📌 Why do people ring the bell?

A: For attention.

III-2

📌 What can guests do in the room?

A: To watch TV or for reading.

📌 What time can they use the room?

A: From 10:00am to 10:00pm.

III-3

📌 When people want to open the door, what do they need to do?

A: To press the button.

III-4

📌 When do people keep door closed?

A: At all times.

III-5

📌 What does the sign mean?

A: To ask for cleaning up the room.

📌 Where is the sign usually used?

A: In hotels. Or, by your mother.

III-6

📌 What does the sign mean?

A: To tell other people not to knock the door or enter the room.

📌 Where is the sign used?

A: In hotels. Or, by child that doesn't want to be disturbed.

III-7

📌 What is Bed & Breakfast abbreviated?

A: B & B.

📌 What is the name of the B & B?

A: Willowbank Cottage.

📌 What kind of bedrooms does it provide?

A: Suite.

📌 **What does Willowbank look like?**

    A: A cottage.

📌 **How special is it?**

    A: It has sea views.

📌 **What does No Vacancies mean?**

    A: All suites are full.

III-8

📌 **When is the check-in time?**

    A: At three.

● **When is the check-out time on Sundays?**

    A: At six.

III-9

📌 **Who can guests leave their luggage with?**

    A: The hotel.

📌 **Who is responsible for personal belongings?**

    A: The guests themselves.

III-10

📌 **Who is the note given to?**

    A: The guests.

📌 **What is the note for?**

    A: To help less fortunate people.

III-11

📌 What is the sign for?

A: Encourage people to drink more water.

📌 What features does the tap water have?

A: It's free, clean and drinkable.

III-12

📌 What is the sign for?

A: Reuse the towel to go easy on the planet.

III-13

📌 What things cannot throw in the bin?

A: Bottles.

III-14

📌 What features does the hand wash have?

A: Softly clean hands without drying them out.

📌 What kind of ingredients does the hand wash have?

A: Vegan ingredients infused with a fresh fragrance.

III-15

📌 What does the sign mean?

A: The thing is for hair and body use.

III-16

📌 Where does the arrow point to?

A: To a public restroom.

📌 Where is the public restroom?

A: In the lower deck of the restaurant.

III-17

📌 What does the roof have?

A: Many steps.

📌 How are those steps?

A: They may be slippery.

📌 What activities are not allowed to do there?

A: Bicycles and skateboard.

📌 Who will take the responsibility, if someone plays skateboard games and gets hurt?

A: He/she will be at his/her own risk.

III-18

📌 Where can people see the sign?

A: at the restaurant

📌 What do people do when they see the sign?

A: They need to wait for being seated. Or, they cannot go to find the table by themselves.

III-19

📌 How much does it cost if the customer orders fajita taco and chalupa?

A: 4.24

📌 How much is it for the to-go tea?

A: 1.69

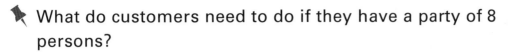

📌 What do customers need to do if they have a party of 8 persons?

    A: They will be charged a 15% gratuity.

III-20

📌 What kind of food is on the menu?

    A: American food.

📌 What kinds of hamburgers does it serve?

    A: Regular hamburger, cheeseburger, and double meat cheeseburger.

📌 What will be served with dinner?

    A: French fries or mashed potatoes, Texas toast, and gravy.

III-21

📌 What meal is on the menu?

    A: Salads.

📌 What will be served if the customer orders chef salad?

    A: Chicken strips.

📌 What kind of salad dressings are there?

    A: Ranch, thousand island, and French.

III-22

📌 What kind of food is on the menu?

    A: Mexican food.

📌 What will be served with Mexican plates?

    A: Rice, refried beans, and salad.

📌 What will be included for beef fajita dinner?

    A: Pico de gallo, guacamole, and 2 tortillas.

III-23

📌 What's the name of the restaurant?

    A: Ale House.

📌 Which appetizer will be served with gorgonzola dipping sauce?

    A: Buffalo wings.

📌 What will Portabella mushroom be stuffed with?

    A: Spinach, artichoke and gorgonzola.

📌 If customers order west Texas white queso, what thing will be served?

    A: Tortilla chips.

III-24

📌 Which speciality will be served with tartar sauce?

    A: Beer tempura battered fish and chips.

📌 What ingredients does Thai Red Curry include?

    A: Chicken, snow peas, broccoli, red bell pepper, shiitake, and mushrooms.

📌 Which speciality will be served with Japanese marinated cucumbers?

    A: Seared tuna.

📌 What do they have for the dish of Spicy Herb Roasted Chicken?

    A: Half chicken, twice baked fried potato balls, and vegetable of the day.

III-25

📌 What may the customers have at the end of the meal?

    A: Free coffee.

📌 **Where can the customers scan the QR code?**

A: At the bottom of the page.

📌 **What do the customers need to do after accessing to the website?**

A: Complete a survey.

📌 **What message do the customers show the server?**

A: Thanking for participating.

III-26

📌 **What meal is served on the menu?**

A: Breakfast.

📌 **Which is the most expensive dish?**

A: Briske & Chorizo Hash.

📌 **What food will be served if the customer orders baked fresh daily?**

A: Cinnamon rolls, assorted scones, and muffins.

III-27

📌 **What meal is served on the menu?**

A: Lunch.

📌 **How much will the customer pay if they order 8 buffalo wings?**

A: 9 dollars.

📌 **Which dish is the cheapest one?**

A: The manor burger.

III-28

🔖 What do they serve for the desserts?

A: Slice of cake or pie.

🔖 How much is the cup of soup?

A: 2 dollars.

🔖 How will signature chicken salad be served?

A: In a sandwich or over a bed of lettuce.

🔖 How much is it for the bottled water?

A: 1 dollar.

III-29

🔖 Based on Manor Park Policy, what is a customer not allowed to do?

A: Tipping.

🔖 If customers are having undercooked meats or raw seafood, what will they risk?

A: Food borne illness.

🔖 Why does Manor Park feel proud of?

A: By using pasteurized eggs.

Part 4 | Road Signs 路標

IV-1

🔖 What are people not allowed to do?

A: Dumping and motor vehicle.

📌 Can the cyclist ride on this road?

A: Yes, he/she can.

IV-2

📌 What do drivers do in this area?

A: To load or unload things.

📌 When do the drivers need to use the flasher in this area?

A: When they need to take 15 minutes to load or unload things.

IV-3

📌 What does the sign mean?

A: Drivers are prohibited from driving past the sign.

IV-4

📌 What does the sign mean?

A: The driver can only drive out.

📌 What does 'exit' mean?

A: 'Exit' means 'go out' oppose to 'enter' means 'come in'.

IV-5

📌 What does the sign mean?

A: The vehicles are not allowed to pass beyond the sign.

IV-6

📌 What does the sign mean?

A: The lanes are for bus only.

IV-7

📌 What does the sign mean?

A: Drivers are not allowed to park their cars in the zone, Monday to Friday from 8:30am to 5:30pm.

IV-8

📌 What does the sign mean?

A: Drivers are not allowed to park their cars in the zone, Monday to Saturday from 8:30am to 6:30pm.

IV-9

📌 What is the name of this building?

A: Castle Esplanade

📌 What time is the car park closed?

A: 10:30am~4:30pm

📌 Who are allowed to park?

A: Authorized vehicles

IV-10

📌 What does the sign 'All Traffic MUST Turn Right' mean?

A: All drivers have to turn right.

IV-11

📌 What does the sign mean?

A: Drivers who are on the right land must make a right turn.

IV-12

📌 What can't drivers do when the traffic light is red?

A: They cannot turn when the traffic light is red.

IV-13

🔖 Where is it? .

　　A: It's at South 11th Street.

🔖 What do the drivers need to do in this street?

　　A: They need to make a detour.

IV-14

🔖 What does the sign mean?

　　A: It is on South 11 Street. And, it is the end of detour.

IV-15

🔖 What does it mean when you see this sign?

　　A: There is no exit.

IV-16

🔖 What does the sign mean?

　　A: All vehicles are driven toward the same direction on the road.

IV-17

🔖 What is the sign for?

　　A: To remind the drivers of the speed limit.

🔖 When the drivers see the sign, what do they need to do?

　　A: They need to slow down.

IV-18

🔖 Why do people push the button?

　　A: For walk signal.

🔖 When the walk signal is on, what does it mean?

　　A: Pedestrian can cross the street.

IV-19

What does the sign mean?

A: The weight limit is 8 tons.

IV-20

What does the sign mean?

A: The road is closed ahead.

When the driver sees this sign, what does he/she need to do?

A: The driver has to find another way to drive.

IV-21

When the driver sees 'no right turn ahead', what does he/she need to do?

A: They can't make a right turn ahead.

IV-22

What does the road look like when you see this sign?

A: It is a three-way intersection.

Who needs to be cautious?

A: Pedestrians.

Why?

A: Vehicles coming up the hill do not stop.

IV-23

What does the sign on the top mean?

A: No parking on this side.

What does the sign in the middle mean?

A: It's a bus stop here.

📌 **What does the sign at the bottom mean?**

A: It's a tow-away zone.

IV-24

📌 **Where is the walkway bound?**

A: To Robertshaw and South campus.

IV-25

📌 **What does the sign mean?**

A: It's a crosswalk for the pedestrians. Pedestrians are safe in this community.

IV-26

📌 **What does the driver need to do, when he/she sees the sign above?**

A: They need to slow down or stop their cars, and watch out for pedestrians.

📌 **Who can park, based on the sign below?**

A: Staff.

IV-27

📌 **What zone is it?**

A: A walk zone. You can only walk.

📌 **In what situation, what activities are not allowed to do in this zone?**

A: When pedestrians are present, cycling and skateboarding are prohibited in the zone.

IV-28

📌 What does the sign mean?

A: To warn road users about level crossing with no barriers.

📌 What do the drivers need to do when they see the sign?

A: They need to slow down.

IV-29

📌 When can people board?

A: When the departure is called.

📌 Why does a train cause injury?

A: The train rolls.

IV-30

📌 When the drivers are at the railroad crossing, what do they need to do?

A: They need to stop, look, and listen before they cross the road.

📌 How many tracks does the sign indicate?

A: Two.

IV-31

📌 Why do people need to keep themselves from the railroad tracks?

A: For the sake of safety.

📌 What do people need to stay away from, and how far?

A: They need to stay away from railroad tracks at least 20 feet.

IV-32

📌 What may happen if persons are on or near track?

A: They may have serious injury.

📌 If accidents or injuries happen, who will be responsible?

A: The persons who are on or near track cause the accidents or injuries by themselves. Or, people who doesn't follow the warning.

IV-33

📌 What are passengers not allowed to do in the train?

A: Smoking, spitting, and adjusting heater or air conditioning.

📌 Where do passengers stay when they are taking the train?

A: They have to stay seated at all times.

📌 What kinds of passengers will be ejected from the train?

A: Unruly passengers.

📌 What animals can ride without ticket?

A: Service animals.

IV-34

📌 What is the name of the park?

A: Alameda Park.

📌 When was it founded?

A: It was established in 1898.

📌 When are its opening hours?

A: It opens from 7:00am to 10:00pm.

IV-35

🔖 What does the sign mean?

A: To warn people not to enter.

🔖 Who owns the property?

A: The city of Alamogordo

🔖 If people don't follow the sign, what will happen?

A: They will be prosecuted.

IV-36

🔖 What does the sign mean?

A: The place will be closed at dusk and people are not allowed to enter after that.

🔖 When will the place close?

A: At dusk.

🔖 Where is the place located?

A: The city of Alamogordo.

IV-37

🔖 What activities can't people do?

A: Skating, skateboarding, and bicycling are prohibited.

🔖 How many persons can be on the swing at a time?

A: One.

IV-38

🔖 When are the city parks open?

A: From dawn to 10:30pm.

🔖 When can't people stay in the parks?

A: From 10:30pm to dawn.

IV-39

🔖 How are vehicles allowed to park?

A: With permit.

🔖 How do drivers get permits?

A: They can call at 439-4142.

IV-40

🔖 What basis is facility use on?

A: First come first serve.

🔖 Who can have exception?

A: People with permitted reservations.

🔖 How to get a permit?

A: Call the Alamogordo family recreation center at 4394142.

IV-41

🔖 What does the sign mean?

A: People are not allowed to drink alcoholic beverages in public places.

🔖 What is the rule based on?

A: It's based on City Ordinance # 5-01-050.

🔖 What is the title of the rule?

A: Drinking in Public Places.

IV-42

📌 What does this sign mean?

A: It reminds people of being cautious with their money and specific persons.

📌 What kinds of people are mentioned in this sign?

A: The pickpockets and loose women.

IV-43

📌 Who asks pet owners to do something for their pets?

A: The city ordinance.

📌 What do pet owners need to do to their pets in the park?

A: The owners need to leash and clean up after their pets.

📌 What problems does the pet waste cause?

A: The pet waste is a threat to the health of children, degrades town, and transmits disease.

IV-44

📌 What does the sign mean?

A: The pet owners have to clean up after their pet.

📌 What is the maximum penalty?

A: 500 pounds.

Part 5 | Campus Life 校園生活

V-1

📌 What do people need to do if they need to use the elevator?

A: They can call on phone.

📌 Where is the phone located?

A: It is located by front doors to Wallace dormitory.

📌 How to use the phone?

A: Open black box, push black button, and dial.

V-2

📌 Who is the campus sidewalks closed to?

A: The public.

📌 Why is the campus sidewalks closed?

A: Construction.

V-3

📌 How do the disabled gain access to the building?

A: They can do it at the rear of the building.

V-4

📌 What time will the office be closed?

A: At 4:30pm.

📌 What are the similarity and difference between office hours and summer hours?

A: They are open at the same time in the morning from 8:00am to 12:00 noon. The opening and closing hours are different in the afternoon. One is from 1:00pm to 4:30pm. The other is from 12:30pm to 4:00pm.

V-5

📌 What are three recycling items?

A: Plastic bottles, drinks cans, and paper.

📌 **Why do people recycle?**

A: To protect the environment and save energy.

V-6

📌 **Why does the window only open 100mm?**

A: For people's health and safety.

📌 **What does the sign mean?**

A: Warn people not to try and force the window to open further or disengage the restrictor.

📌 **If people break or damage the window, what will happen to them?**

A: They will be charged for the damage.

V-7

📌 **Why do people need to be quiet?**

A: A show is in progress.

📌 **Who can access to the show?**

A: The authorized only.

V-8

📌 **Where are additional restrooms?**

A: They are on the first floor.

V-9

📌 **Where are the restrooms located?**

A: They are near the staircases and on the first floor.

📌 **Where are the staircases?**

A: They are on both of the right and left hand sides.

V-10

🖈 Who does the sign remind of?

A: The last one to leave.

🖈 How to conserve energy?

A: To turn off the lights.

🖈 Who made this sign?

A: UW Facilities Services Department.

V-11

🖈 What does the sign mean?

A: To ask people not to smoke in this area.

V-12

🖈 What can't people use when a building is on fire?

A: The elevators.

🖈 What can people use when they cannot use elevators?

A: The stairways.

🖈 What will be out of service during emergencies?

A: The elevators.

V-13

🖈 When do people lock the door and arm the alarm on weekdays and weekends?

A: They do it after 7:00pm on weekdays and at all times on weekends.

V-14

🖈 Where can people smoke?

A: In designated areas.

V-15

Where are journals not permitted in?

A: Study carrels and upper floor of the library.

Where is the study carrel?

A: In the library.

V-16

Why do people need to be respectful of others in the zone?

A: It is a quiet study zone.

V-17

Where do people need to limit their cell phone use?

A: On the first and ground floors of the library.

Where is the ground floor in a building?

A: It is under the first floor.

V-18

What time is the restroom cleaned?

A: Between 10:30 and 11:00am.

If people need to use the restroom during cleaning time, what do they need to do?

A: They can use the restroom on another floor.

V-19

In what situation, people are allowed to take the exit?

A: In an emergency.

What happens if people use the exit?

A: The alarm will sound.

V-20

🖈 What drinks are permitted to have?

    A: Covered drinks.

🖈 What food is permitted to have?

    A: Java City food.

V-21

🖈 What things are not allowed to be removed from this floor?

    A: Journals.

🖈 What can't people do with the journals on this floor?

    A: They cannot take journals to other floors.

V-22

🖈 What does germ-buster mean?

    A: Germ killer/exterminator.

🖈 How to stay away from germ?

    A: Wash hands.

🖈 After washing hands, how do people turn off water?

    A: With paper towel.

🖈 What are the steps of washing hands?

    A: Wet, soap, wash, rinse, dry and turn off water with paper towel.

V-23

🖈 Who is this sign for?

    A: For faculty, staff and students.

🖈 What might people do when they see the sign?

    A: To get a free flu shot.

📌 **How much do people pay for the shots?**

A: They are free for faculty, staff, and students.

📌 **Where do people go to take the shot?**

A: In the student union MB2110 (old game room).

📌 **What do people need to bring with them for the shots?**

A: Current UTPB ID.

V-24

📌 **Based on the sign, how do people stay healthy?**

A: Cover cough and wash hands.

📌 **When people want to cough or sneeze, what do they need to do?**

A: Cover their mouth and nose with a tissue. Or, they cough or sneeze into their upper sleeve.

📌 **How do people clean their hands?**

A: They wash their hands with soap and warm water. Or, they can clean their hands with alcohol-based hand cleaner.

 MEMO

國家圖書館出版品預行編目資料

實用英文/陳愛華, 張景翔編著. -- 初版. -- 新北市：
新文京開發出版股份有限公司, 2021.05
　　面；　　公分

ISBN　978-986-430-720-3（平裝）

1. 英語　2. 讀本

805.18　　　　　　　　　　　　　　　110006244

實用英文　　　　　　　　　　　　　　（書號：E447）

編　　　者	陳愛華　張景翔
出　版　者	新文京開發出版股份有限公司
地　　　址	新北市中和區中山路二段 362 號 9 樓
電　　　話	(02) 2244-8188（代表號）
F　A　X	(02) 2244-8189
郵　　　撥	1958730-2
初　　　版	西元 2021 年 08 月 10 日

有著作權　不准翻印　　　　　　建議售價：400 元

法律顧問：蕭雄淋律師

ISBN　978-986-430-720-3

New Wun Ching Developmental Publishing Co., Ltd.

New Age · New Choice · The Best Selected Educational Publications — NEW WCDP

新文京開發出版股份有限公司

NEW
WCDP

新世紀・新視野・新文京 — 精選教科書・考試用書・專業參考書